WRITING
DOCUMENTARY & FILM SCRIPT

PG PUBLICATION

Delhi - 110089 (India)

Edition : 2020

ISBN : 978-93-89984-39-2

Price : Rs. 499/-

Writing documentary & film script
by
Yash Singhania & Ishita Vyas

Cover page
Praveen Kasana

Published by
PRAKHAR GOONJ PUBLICATION
H-3/2, Sector - 18, Rohini, Delhi - 110089
Contact : 7982710571, 7838505899, 011-27851059
Email : prakhargoonj@gmail.com,
sinha.neelu123@gmail.com

Writing

DOCUMENTARY & FILM SCRIPT

Writeen By

Yash Singhania

&

Ishita Vyas

Dedicated to . . .

Shri Anjum Rajabali
(Veteran Indian Screenwriter)

Shri Subhash Ghai
(Founder - Whistling Woods International School)

Shri Sandeep Marwah
(Asian Academy of Film & Television, Noida)

PREFACE

Here's something people often forget: it takes a person to write movies. Screenwriting involves writing down ideas so that they'll be easily translated into visual art. A screenplay, or script, is the backbone of any movie. It's the first step in the moviemaking process. Almost everybody on the movie set has a copy of the script because it reveals what they should be doing. It tells the actors how to act and what to say, the production designer how to build the set, and the director how to shoot the scene.

A good script has many facets (fame, fortune, love, marriage, affairs, divorce, despair, and so on); choose the ones you want. However, screenplays have their own language, their own slang, if you will.

Before You Start...

At the outset, you must realize that screenwriting is a competitive sport. The Film Writers Association of India registers over 5,000 scripts a year, and less than 1% of them are made into motion pictures. Everyone in India and every second person elsewhere has a script they're trying to sell, so your chances as a beginner are slim to none.

And fame shouldn't be a factor in your decision either. Not only does the public at large never bother to find out who wrote a film, but the major Film producers often show the same lack of respect toward screenwriters. But if you are passionate about writing, about movies, and about making your dreams come true, then you should seriously consider writing for the movies. When you think about it, screenwriting is the toughest job in Bollywood. The screenwriter is the only person on a film crew who starts with absolutely nothing. That said, let's write this baby.

First of all, you need to find a story that interests you. Wipe those illusions away, it's all been done before; the trick is to develop your story in a new and original way. Start with a concept you can describe in a sentence such as: Considering a screenplay is between 90 and 120 pages long (one page averages one minute of screen time), you must have enough material so your story can be interesting for the duration. You must ask yourself questions while developing your story. What happens then? Who does it happen to? Why? As you answer these questions, you will discover new twists to your story and, before long, you'll be ready to write it.

Before you can call it quits on your first screenplay, there are some things you must look out for. Readers won't have a problem if they only run across a couple of typos in the entire script. But if there are dozens per page, it will be an indication to them that you're sloppy and didn't put much effort into it. It's often enough for them to stop reading altogether. Proofread meticulously.

As a neophyte, the type of screenplay you're writing is called a "spec"; it's meant as a calling card, a proof of your talents. Spec scripts by beginners are rarely produced, so lay off camera directions. As arbitrary as some of the format and presentation rules may appear, it's absolutely fundamental that you comply with those guidelines with minimal deviation. Follow these principles and instead focus your imagination on crafting a terrific story.

Screenwriting is a creative job. You must not be stubborn in trying to develop a story in only one way. Explore different avenues and see if you can make your characters come to life and dictate where your storyline should go.

Your first screenplay will likely be terrible — but don't worry, the more you try, the better you'll get at it.

- Yash Singhania & Ishita Vyas

TABLE OF CONTENTS

PART - I : Documentary Screenplay

PART - II : Film Screenplay

PART-I

D O C U M E N T A R Y S C R E E N P L A Y

1
FADE IN :

"Writing a screenplay is like climbing a mountain. When you're climbing, all you can see is the rock in front of you and the rock directly above you. You can't see where you've come from or where you're going."

Syd Field (Screenwriting Lecturer)

Introduction

Gene Fowler once said that writing is easy, just a matter of staring at a blank page until your forehead bleeds. Well, if anything will draw blood from your forehead, it's writing a brilliant documentary script!

Often in our real lives, ideas and emotions, mind and passion, revolve in different spheres altogether. On film, if we see a dead body, we react immediately with emotion, perhaps even pondering the waste of life and questioning our own existence. However, if we were to see a dead body on a street as we drove by, our immediate reaction may be shock, even revulsion. Emotion may enter the picture long after the experience has ended. In *real* life, experiences become meaningful with reflection in time. In *reel* life, they are meaningful the moment they happen. A well-written film script is an instrument through which you can create emotion and epiphany at will. That is one reason why it is possibly the most critical aspect of the filmmaking procedure.

The script is also, often, the most underrated aspect of the documentary process. A school of thought suggests that the documentary-making process should be fluid and organic, whereby the filmmaker experiences the film as he makes it. Many filmmakers write a 'paper-edit' after shooting in place of a script. This process has and does work with many types of films. Especially when the filmmaker is recording events beyond his control like political rallies, events, natural disasters, riots and demonstrations etc. However, in most films, the filmmaker will find himself asking the question, "What should I shoot?" Here, it is imperative to start out with a well-written script, *whether or not things change during the shooting process*. Often preparing a script beforehand can make the difference between a bad film and a good film. Or, at best, a good film and a great film.

There are two stages of documentary scriptwriting:

(i) The Pre-shoot or Shooting Script

(ii) The Post-shoot Script

A **pre-shoot or shooting script** is like carrying a map when you set out on a road trip. You may stumble across many unseen barriers or unexpected surprises. You may discover wonderful, uncharted areas off the beaten track. You may decide to go in one direction or the next or perhaps even a third. A map helps you on your way and prevents you from getting lost. A shooting script is a conceptual map for your shooting journey. It consolidates research and outlines the film's story, providing a visual guideline for the shoot. It uses the same format and elements as a post-shoot script and can be as comprehensive or generic depending on the information available to the scriptwriter at that stage.

A shooting script should not be confused with a shot list. A shot list is a production tool which contains shot numbers, descriptions and transitions along with production details. Even though some director-scriptwriters often combine the shooting script and shot list, the two are separate entities. A shooting script rarely delves into detailed aspects of production unless integral to the story. It is more conceptual in nature; descriptive, but leaving room for interpretation.

The **post-shoot script** is the final version of the shooting script. This is often a modified or re-written version of the shooting script and is created between the shooting and editing processes of the documentary. The post-shoot script combines conceptual elements along with audiovisual information gathered at the production stage and may also include any new knowledge gathered along the way. It then weaves it all together into a cinematic story, which is used by the filmmaker to edit the documentary. The postshoot script often includes descriptions of shots and actions and is quite comprehensive.

Again, the post-shoot script should not be confused with a paper-edit, which contains detailed shot and production information. Even though the two are often combined by director-scriptwriters, they are separate entities. The paper-edit is a tool for the editor to cut the footage and includes elements like time-counters, tape numbers, shot in-points and out-points etc. The script is conceptual and descriptive of action but should leave some room for creative interpretation at the editing stage.

Both the pre-shoot and post-shoot scripts are time-specific versions of the same entity. The same elements and technique can be used to create both depending on the amount of information available at that time.

◆ ◆ ◆

2

Why Writing for Films and Documentaries are different

Writing for film, fiction or non-fiction, is quite different from writing for print. There are a few unique features of film that a screenwriter must consider:

- ***Film is visual.*** The words that a screenwriter writes will never be read by anyone. They will only be seen and heard as images on a screen. The most important skill of a screenwriter is that he must be able to write visually. Theorizing or explaining a concept in a script is pointless; if the audience can't 'look' at the theory, it's not worth writing. A screenwriter must think, 'Is what I'm about to write visual in nature? If not, then how can I make it visual?"
- ***Film shows motion***. Most of the images you see on screen have action. It's what separates moving images from photographs. Stories for film must be translated by a screenwriter into active images.
- ***Film reveals what the eye often can't see.*** A tiny cell in our bodies, a country we've never been to, details that we would normally miss. The screenwriter must bring things to life for the audience who may have never before experienced what they see on screen.
- ***Film transcends time and space.*** A film doesn't adhere to our dimensions of time and space. Once made, it continues to exist in a little bubble of its own, transcending

the limits of our present lives. A screenwriter must understand that writing for a film means creating a being that should have a life of its own long after the writer has moved on from it.

• ***Film is Subjective.*** By simply pointing the camera in a specific direction, a subjective choice has been made. The very nature of film, like our eyes, is to focus on what is considered to be the object of interest and eliminate what lies beyond the lens, thereby losing all sense of objectivity.

• ***Film chooses audience***. The screenwriter must always keep in mind that each film chooses its own audience depending on how he chooses to tell the story. By varying a script, he may be showing the film to very different people in the end.

• ***Film repeats accurately.*** Film footage doesn't discriminate between objects, doesn't hide, cheat or lie. It consistently reproduces what the camera sees in full detail. It is the filmmaker who must shoot objects in a particular way to include or eliminate details.

• ***Film may have colour and audio elements.*** It's not only about moving images. Most films, unless the filmmaker chooses not to use them, have the elements of sound and colour. These elements are always, if present, incorporated into the script.

• ***Film emphasizes and emotionalizes.*** Films can evoke different kinds of reactions in the audience, from grief to anger. They can make the audience think and send powerful messages across to them.

When it comes to documentaries in particular, there are a few more things to be kept in mind before starting to write a script. Documentary scripts do share many common elements with scripts for fiction films, shorts and features alike. However, they also have their own specific considerations:

- ***Documentary deals with fact, not fiction.*** Most importantly, documentaries delve into a non-fictional world with real events, real issues, real conflict, real people and real emotions. Everything seen and heard on screen is grounded in accuracy and has no element of fiction.

- ***Documentary is flexible.*** Unlike fictional films, documentaries have no fixed visual and conceptual guidelines per say. It's impossible to concretize events or decide one way or the other about how the film will turn out eventually. There are fewer 'rules' to be followed, which reflects the fact that there are few rules in the real world as well. This makes it more challenging but infinitely more exciting.

- ***Documentary inspires movement and action.*** At the very heart of documentary, there is an issue and a message at hand. The passing on of this message to the audience is usually the reason that the film was made in the first place. Documentaries have long been used as an instrument to inspire change in their audience, be it social change or inner change.

- ***Documentary involves less control.*** Unlike fiction films, documentaries must be shot in the real world and show real events happening. Often, the filmmaker is unable to control the event he is shooting as well as the circumstances surrounding the event. It's difficult to think about lighting when in the middle of a sniper shootout! There is less control over the subject in documentary; however this unmodified, improvised element is often the very charm of non-fiction films.

- ***Documentary subject is paramount.*** Documentaries are inherently bound to their subject matter. Since their purpose is so issue-specific and their circumstances are non-fictional, the subject is the most important aspect of documentary films and is given precedence over other aspects, for example: entertainment value. In fact, until recently filmmakers scoffed at the idea of a documentary being entertaining. This attitude has, of course, changed now but subject still remains the dominant element.

• ***Credibility is key in Documentary.*** The emergence of the documentary as a recognised cinematic genre in the 1920's inherited the trust of the audience in the veracity of the image as an authentic representation of the real. Today, we are much more skeptical, even with documentaries. Audience trust, once lost is gone forever so a documentary, in this day and age, must always provide credible information and sources to put a suspicious audience at ease.

• ***Form is more important than formula.*** There are no recipes in documentary films. Every subject and issue is specific and is showcased on film in its own appropriate manner. Form and the layout in which a subject is showcased in a film are important as they add value to the film, but there is no one tried and tested way to do this.

In addition to these conceptual considerations, the screenwriter must ask a number of practical questions as well:

• *Why is this film being made?*

• *What does the producer/client/financier want to achieve through the film?*

• *Who is the targeted audience and what should their reaction to the film be?*

• *How much does the audience already know about the subject?*

• *What will be the film's technical conditions of use (Black & White/Multi-colour? Animation? Etc)*

• *What is the budget of the film?*

These factors contribute significantly to the nature of the script for the simple reason that, at the end of the day, film like any other art is a product. Artistry must go hand in hand with practicality, production technicalities and, of course, economics. You may ask yourself, “What difference does a film’s budget make to a script?” The answer is, enormous.

It would be easy to write a powerful scene about an ancient battle in a foreign country but the reality of it is that the film crew would have to fly there, hire hundreds of men, use elaborate costumes and props and perhaps even hire trained horses for authenticity. There would even be the additional costs of transport, food etc.

This could be an expense the budget does not allow. The scriptwriter will probably have to write a ‘cheaper’ version of the same scene, which might be to shoot abstract visuals of a few men’s feet running, weapons clashing, bloody faces etc and supplement them with the voice of an historian talking about the battle in question and what happened in it.

Less elaborate? Certainly. Less powerful? Not necessarily.

◆ ◆ ◆

3

Short Introduction to Documentary styles

Over the years, several documentary styles evolved that came and went from fashion. These styles ranged from newsreel to realist to romantic to propaganda and many more. However, three emerged as the most popular and encompassed most of the documentary films made well up to the 1990's.

Classical Cinema

This is the most structured and traditional form of documentary. It gives great importance to clarity of narrative and images. Characters drive the plots, and continuity editing ensures the seamless progression of events. These kinds of documentaries often made extensive use of didactic narration, as was seen in the most famous documentary in this style, *Night Mail* by John Grierson, which showed, in dramatised detail, how mail was transported by train overnight. The sequences were tightly controlled and the 'feel' was quite formal. The element of 'realism' was often interfered with by the filmmaker, who interspersed on-location shots with studio shots and sound dubbing to show real events and make them more 'filmable'.

Cinéma Vérité / Direct Cinema

This style of documentary originated in the late 1950's and reached new heights of popularity in the 1960's. It was, much like the generation that pioneered it, a rebel with a cause. This style was spurred on with the advancement of film technology, including portable cameras with mobile sound. Cinéma Vérité, meaning

'True Cinema' in French, aimed for an extreme naturalism, using non-professional actors, non-intrusive filming techniques, a hand-held camera, genuine locations rather than sound stages, and naturalistic sound without post-production or voiceovers. The camera was a 'fly on the wall' and took in everything that went on before it. This broke all the rules put into practice by the classical tradition. Direct Cinema and Cinéma Vérité are often used interchangeably, although there are opinions that make distinctions by the degree of camera involvement. The fundamentals of style, however, are very similar between the two. Famous cinéma vérité/direct cinema films include *Showman*, *Salesman*, *The Children Were Watching*, *Primary*, *Behind a Presidential Crisis*, and *Grey Gardens*.

Documentary Drama

This style mixes the techniques of drama and the factual elements of documentary. Real events are acted out by professional actors in controlled settings in an obviously constructed style. This theatrical retelling of facts began in the early days of broadcasting when practical concerns and unwieldy equipment made it difficult to shoot live events. However, it is used even today. Most modern documentaries include some form of event recreation. The popular UK television show, *Coronation Street*, was originally thought of as a drama documentary.

The docu-drama style has been one of the most controversial ones till date and many have questioned whether it is a documentary style at all. Contention arose because, while documentaries are thought to be "real", docu-dramas were thought to cheat by obviously reconstructing reality. This opinion has been more or less discarded now as most people not only accept the diminishing lines of distinction between different styles of film, but also the overall artificiality of the subsequent editing process for all styles.

These days, with the advent of documentary films into the worldwide commercial film arena as well as their ever-expanding production in most countries of the world, most generic classifications of style have been put to rest. New stylistic elements are experimented with every year and the lines between genres have been crossed so many times that specific categories are impossible to define. Reality TV, for example, has stormed the world of television, taking direct cinema to new levels of voyeurism. Whether they are wobbly, out-of-focus home video diaries or the 'making-of-a-feature' promotional films included in DVD packs, they have all served to broaden our definition of the traditional documentary.

So how does all this concern the scriptwriter of a documentary film? This evolution, leading to the overlap of styles and genres, has placed far more overt, interpretive control in the hands of the filmmaker and, consequently, in the hands of the scriptwriter. Before embarking on the writing process, it is important to know the various stylistic options available to you as a scriptwriter. It is also important to recognize the contribution of various traditional styles to modern ones, even if their only use is as a guide to finding a style and 'voice' of your own.

◆ ◆ ◆

4

RESEARCH, RESEARCH, RESEARCH YOU CAN`T SAY IT ENOUGH!

Every film, especially a documentary, has a 'value'. This could be social, political, historical, philosophical, artistic or of some other kind. The amount of research a scriptwriter puts in is directly related to the 'value' of the film.

In the rush to get started, many people often skim over the research process. Especially in films that involve subjects of a personal nature; for example: a person's journey within his own family to explore social dynamics. A scriptwriter could be instructed to write a script on a live event that was shot some time ago, like a riot, or for a film on the thoughts and feelings of a celebrity already captured in detail on camera.

He might ask himself, "How can I possibly add anything more to the subject information?" Even in films that seem straightforward and detailed information has already been given to the scriptwriter, there is always room for more research. There are simply no shortcuts that will provide the quality of a well-researched film.

Suppose a scriptwriter has the footage of a live riot, shot by the filmmaker, along with a detailed log of the events that took place before, during and afterwards, the filmmaker's personal thoughts about his experience and on-camera interviews with people on both sides about their views.

He may think he has enough information to write a fairly

comprehensive script and he would be right. However, what if he did a little study on the political, historical and social reasons why that riot may have taken place for some extra context, or if he spoke to a few more people who were involved on that day and who may have seen something he didn't know about. Perhaps he could visit the riot site, or meet an expert on riots and get his perspective on what happened and even collect the newspaper coverage of that riot and think about the role of media in that event.

He could even go so far as to place himself in the middle of a riot (highly unadvisable) to get a first-hand perspective on the experience. In the end, he may or may not use any of the so-called 'extra' information he gathered, but his in-depth knowledge on the subject would be extremely valuable in creating an insightful and engaging script.

Curiosity

The best research is done when there is a genuine desire on the part of the scriptwriter to learn more about the subject of his documentary.

This is easier said than done, especially when you get that dreaded call about writing a script on the inner components of a diesel generator, but inspiration and curiosity go a long way in helping a scriptwriter. After all, if you're not excited about it, how on earth are you going to make hundreds, thousands or even millions of people excited? Therefore, the first step in the research process would be to develop a healthy interest and curiosity about the subject of the film.

The scriptwriter must ask himself some important questions:

- What have I not yet been told about this subject?
- Is everything I have been told the truth? How much do I need to verify?
- What would I personally like to know about this subject?
- If I were a member of the audience, what would I want to learn about this subject?

- What can I find that is little known on this subject?
- If the shooting has not yet started, what information can I gather that would aid the filming process?

Quantity Vs Quality

One of the more important questions that scriptwriters have is, "How much research is enough?" The quality of research is far more important than the quantity. After all, if you were a writing a script for a film on the First World War, you could spend a lifetime studying the subject and never meet that script deadline. One of the more important skills of the scriptwriter is to segregate relevant information from the irrelevant.

This can be done by having detailed and on-going communication with the filmmaker at all times. The focus of the film and the subject matter it is dealing with must be kept in mind at all times. Any information gathered or lead followed must first be put through a 'relevancy test'.

The scriptwriter must ask himself:

- Is this information or source of information directly related to the subject of my film?
- Is it necessary for the audience to know this information?
- Will this information add to the overall quality of the film?
- Even if it is relevant and will add value, is it *more* relevant than all the other information I have gathered so far?
- Will I be able to incorporate this information into the script even if it is relevant to the subject?

The 'Strategy'

Almost every scriptwriter starts off with a research strategy. After all, it's extremely inconvenient to be in the middle of writing a script when a new piece of information crops up. It's important to think about and list down every approach and every source you will use to gather information needed for research. The all-important question that usually crops up is, "Where do I look?"

Each scriptwriter has his own sources and approaches for gathering information and many use the same tried and tested ways throughout their careers. A few places to start are:

- ***Print Research :***

  There are millions of places to look in print: Newspapers, books, magazines, journals, digests, reports, archives, diaries…the list is endless. The scriptwriter must decide which one will be suitable for subject-related information gathering and then physically get hold of the required publication.

  The usual places to go for finding print material are libraries, bookstores, institutions and organizations with archives and, of course, the internet. Other places could be antique book stores, publishing houses and academic institutions. People also keep print material in their houses and that out-of-print, obscure thesis you were looking for could be lying in your neighbour's house so it never hurts to ask around.

  Unless your film is about something extremely specific, chances are you'll have a stack of a hundred relevant publications lying in your house waiting to be read. Chances also are you'll probably not have enough time to read all of them.

  The art of scouring through large amounts of print material quickly can only be picked up over time, however a novice scriptwriter should try and train his eye to skim over words and stop to read bits of text which occur to him as something he could put in his script or which sounds interesting and should be kept aside. It also helps to keep a look out for 'keywords' or words that strike a chord because of their meaning. These words can be used later on in the script, if you are going to write narration.

  In addition, you may be exploring the idea of including

visuals of print material in your film as well, in which case you must select and isolate this material carefully for filming later.

- ***Field Research :***

Since film is a visual medium, it is integral that a scriptwriter get an accurate picture of the visual information in the film. He could go to the various locations in which the film will be shot, or to locations where events took place earlier or will take place in the future.

The scriptwriter could attend related events or even put himself into places where the people in the film will be or would have been. He could even go to museums, art galleries or any kind of public viewing space where he could gather information. The 'field' exists only in relation to the subject of the film and therefore the options are endless and should be visited upon the scriptwriter's discretion.

Once the writer reaches a location, it is important to look out for things which might be relevant to the script. You could track events as they happened or look for clues that could reveal facts much like a detective. How to gather field material when on location is subjective to the film, but the scriptwriter must keep a look out for all things visual that can be incorporated as images within the script.

The culture of the area should be learnt, the people met, the details noted. Once you gather this knowledge, you must keep it aside for future reference. It also helps when on a shooting location, to note things like where the sunlight comes from at what time and what the sounds are heard around the area. These little details will help you design the script in a more artistic and insightful way.

- ***Interview Research :***

Nine times out of ten, a scriptwriter will be called upon to write a script about something he knows nothing about. Factual knowledge can usually be easily attained from print and field research; however the scriptwriter must also gather perspective. Not one but many. The best way to gain perspective is to speak to people directly and indirectly connected with the subject. Films are a medium for people, by people and therefore a human perspective is imperative for any film.

Interview research, which is basically meeting people and asking them questions, is a must for every film.

The scriptwriter must first decide whom to speak to and what to ask them. Normally, the first person or people to seek out are the experts on the subject at hand. They can provide the scriptwriter with not only knowledge but the benefit of their experience.

If there are specific events in the film, then the scriptwriter can speak to people who were involved with the events, directly and indirectly. The selection of people should be varied to get different, even opposing, types of information from each.

The questions to ask them should cover a range of ideas and should typically include factual and emotional elements as well as opinions and insights. These conversations should be recorded carefully and relevant points should be kept aside. It always helps to listen to any ideas they may have about how you can 'treat' the film conceptually, irrespective of whether you incorporate their opinions into the script or not. Who knows? Somebody may give you a gem of an idea.

•Inner Worlds & Metaphors :

Every scriptwriter has a different personality, a different perspective. Consequently, every scriptwriter has something unique to contribute to a film. This is often one reason why filmmakers come to a specific writer to write their scripts again and again.

Imagination is the biggest talent and tool of the scriptwriter. Although not for everybody, a very effective approach at the research stage can be to look within oneself and gather the benefits of past experiences and try and create an emotional stance on the matter at hand. On a spiritual level, meditating upon the inner world within oneself can be a powerful way of harnessing knowledge locked within the sub-conscious mind and perhaps, if one believes so, the power of the collective unconscious or the cosmos.

Metaphors or parallels exist all around us in our lives. Sometimes, we see something that reminds us of something else or inspires us in a particular way. It could be completely unrelated to the object or concept it invokes a memory of, but still portray it in a meaningful way. You could see a highway ridden with rush hour traffic and be reminded of thousands of ants filing in an out of an anthill carrying food. Or the same sight, with horns blaring and drivers swearing, could make you think about the conquest of a robotic age over humaneness.

The possibilities and metaphors around us are endless, just waiting to be picked out by an inventive and imaginative writer.

Digging Deep

Every scriptwriter wants to write a brilliant script and it's a well known fact that some profound investigation needs to be done for this to be accomplished. So what exactly is digging deep and going beyond the facts? What exactly is the scriptwriter looking for and how can it be defined? There are a few ways of looking at these concerns. Suppose a scriptwriter is researching a film on the migratory killer whales or Orcas off the New Zealand coast.

Here is an example of the kinds of research material he might look for:

- ***The 'Top' of the issue***

The top of the issue includes the facts; killer whales and their appearance, migratory patterns and when they go, where are they spotted, their behavior, their sounds, activities, intelligence. The scriptwriter could delve into scientific research being done on the whales by interviewing two marine researchers, lets call them Ted and Sue, a couple who live and work on the New Zealand coast. The writer could find out the history of the Orcas and the role that humans played in it.

Ted and Sue could even take the scriptwriter on a whale observing expedition, where he would experience the whales first hand and also get an idea of what could be shot for the film.

- ***The 'Heart' of the issue***

The scriptwriter could find out more insightful details about the whales as living creatures and fellow mammals. Do they love, do they hate? Why do they beach themselves all together – is it really collective suicide because they mourn their dead like us humans?

What kinds of relationships do they have among each other?

Yes, a mother whale is attached to her calf, but are the aunts, the uncles?

What do they say to each other when they click and whine?

Have Ted and Sue ever come into close contact with any whale?

Did they feel a connection?

How did the whale react to human contact and was it significant in terms of its emotional value?

What did the scriptwriter feel when he looked at a whale for the first time and did he get a sense of the 'spirit' of the creature?

- ***The 'Root' of the issue***

The scriptwriter would find out that the whales have a tragic history because of the excessive whaling that took place in past decades. This tragic and brutal past was because of people, who hunted them almost to extinction. Could their subsequent conservation by people later on be a result of guilt? The scriptwriter could ask what larger role this film could have and the answer might well be to aid in conserving the Orcas for the future by dispelling myths and increasing awareness. This could the message of the film; that everybody needs to get on board to save the killer whale and help them flourish in the oceans.

- ***The 'Branches' of the issue***

The scriptwriter could try and find related issues that would add value to the film. Does the migration of the whales have any effect on the surrounding ecosystems? How about thinking about the spirit of travel or of the ocean itself? Perhaps talk to a person or a group of people who have saved a beached killer whale in the past. Or go in the opposite direction and talk to a person who has killed a killer whale or eaten one. The possibilities of branching out to explore the issue in greater detail are endless. The scriptwriter should then choose which of the details add value to the film.

- ***Finding Challenges***

An issue, when explored in a film, is incomplete when there is nothing introduced that challenges it. The scriptwriter must study the challenges facing the killer whale and their survival as a species. What is being done by people that is hurting their health and causing their numbers to decline, if at all? Are there any challenges put forth by nature that they have to overcome, for instance, like changing temperatures in the waters of the Antarctic? How about large sharks and the threat they pose? Then, the scriptwriter must ask, 'Is it possible for the killer whales to triumph over these challenges?" and "If they can, then how?" and possibly even, "What can people (i.e. the audience) do to help?"

Sifting the rice from the chaff: The Post-it Method

Once you've done all there was to do, gathered every bit of relevant information, followed every interesting lead and asked every insightful question, chances are you'll have more material than you need. At this stage, it's time to start thinking about which bits of information are going to figure in the film. It's time to start ruthlessly eliminating material that just doesn't tell the story. A film lasts for only so long and there are only so many things to be said.

Organizing research into a comprehensive story basically involves cutting and pasting and seeing which bits of material can follow and 'flow' into each other. A good technique is to write down each piece of information in a few words on a post-it or cue card or simply any small piece of paper. For example: one post-it could state "Whales regularly beach themselves in large numbers" and another one could say "Sue looked into the whale's eyes and cried" etc.

Then, stick the post-its in random order on a blank board or wall in columns and rows. After that, the scriptwriter must start a painful process of plucking, discarding and re-sticking until he forms an information chain, which tells the story the writer wants to tell. The only requirement of the story at this stage is that the information must 'flow' and all the futile bits of material are discarded. It's now time to start thinking about writing that script.

◆ ◆ ◆

5

Essential Script Elements

Whereas film has no grammar per say, there are certain 'rules' of usage in cinematic language and *syntax*, or systematic arrangement, orders these rules and the relationships between them.

This syntax has been determined as a result of the usage of film elements over the years and is not necessarily a determinant of them. Film syntax evolved much like a language.

It was an organic development, descriptive rather than prescriptive and constantly changing and evolving. This evolution is still taking place and new thresholds are being pushed by filmmakers everyday. As a basic guide, however, it is important to know these 'rules' even if only to break them.

There are three elements of film 'language' that should be studied by a script writer and incorporated into a script:

1. <u>Visual Elements</u>

The visual elements of film, or what the audience 'sees' on screen is one of the most integral aspects of writing a script. It's important to understand, firstly, how a film is composed structurally from its smallest component. In a script, this is usually a shot.

• ***The Shot***

A shot is a single 'take' on an image. It starts and finishes at a 'cut-point', which is an editing break in the image. A shot is not defined by any particular image, action or event that takes place on screen. It is more a technical concept.

You can have a single shot of a man picking up a paper or two or three of the same thing. It's basically what occurs between two breaks in editing. In a script, a shot is the smallest visual unit of structure.

Action, Action, Action. You can't say it often enough!

There is a reason why film is called 'moving images'. It's what differentiates it from photographs or painting. Technically, a shot may be a structural unit of film language, but what it contains is more important – action. Shots are made of action. Something needs to be 'happening' in a shot for the audience to see – a man walking, a dog barking, a car reversing, a machine working, a river flowing – anything at all that has action, images moving. These actions form events that drive the shot forward to completion.

It's not enough however, just to have random action on screen. The images, the action, the events have to be meaningful. A documentary, like any film, has limited time in which to convey a multitude of things and to tell a story.

Therefore, all the components within the film must be specific and meaningful so as not to waste precious screen time. Each shot has an underlying 'meaning' depending on the nature and arrangement of objects and actions within it. This visual way of communication or language has evolved through the years and has three basic elements:

1. Icon is showing an object or emotion through its likeness – it is what it is and what the audience sees. The signifier represents the signified through similarity to it. For example, a face on screen showing fear is a face showing fear. There are no other meanings, no 'reading between the lines'. This is the most straightforward approach to a shot.

2. Index measures a quality not because it is identical to it (like an icon), but because it has a direct and inherent relationship to it. For example, to show heat, or the idea of heat, as a visual, the shot could show a thermometer or heat waves over an empty road or perhaps even a man sweating profusely. This works very well because the scriptwriter can translate an intangible object, like heat, into a tangible and visual reality.

3. Symbol or **Metaphor** is an arbitrary sign in which the signifier has neither a direct nor an indexical relationship with the signified, but rather represents it through convention. For example, a rose could be shown to signify love or romance, falling calendar pages could denote time.

This technique of using symbols to express ideas and objects has become very popular for its artistic appeal but can and should be used with caution and with a view to the audience's ability to 'read between the lines'.

- ***The Sequence***

  A sequence is a collection of shots put together that tell a story continuously. A sequence is an autonomous piece of the larger story of the film. An entire film is made up of a series of sequences, which can be of varying durations, and are connected to each other in some way. Each sequence has a visual and audio aspect to it.

If a shot is made up of action, a sequence is made up of events. Events mean change in action. These events are built up by the action in the shots to make some sort of sense to the audience and pass along information to them.

Sequences usually fall into one of two categories:

1. A Continuity Sequence is a unit of continuing action which ends in a break in time. This type of sequence is a collection of shots that show an event or events that happened in the same block of time.

The end of the sequence occurs when that event is complete and the film moves on to another point in time. The shots within this kind of sequence must be functional, must be logical and must give the illusion of continuity.

For example, a continuity sequence could be of a man walking from his house to his office. The sequence starts from when he is outside his front door and the first shot could be of him locking it. After that there could be shots of him walking along the street in his neighbourhood, passing people on the street, going past a children's park, walking on a pedestrian path with other office goers and, finally, walking into the entrance of his office building. The shots in this sequence would all appear to be in chronological order and continuous.

2. A Compilation Sequence is a unit of information or thought and is sometimes called a 'newsreel sequence'. There may be many breaks in time during this kind of sequence because the scope is broad. The shots within it could be of events that occurred independently, at different points in time, at different locations and contain different people doing different things. The common aspect that ties all these shots together is conceptual, which is the subject of the sequence.

It usually ends when the film's discussion of the subject ends. For example, the sequence could be about worldwide protests against war and could contain different shots of people from all parts of the globe, some holding banners, some marching hand-in-hand, some giving speeches etc. the sequence would end, when the subject of these protests ended in the film.

A scriptwriter has many choices to make when deciding about the content, treatment and nature of sequences. They can have their own distinct 'personalities'. A sequence can have a completely autonomous audio-visual and conceptual quality to it. A sequence can be a mere chronological aspect within the film, like a link in a chain, without anything distinct about it.

A sequence can be descriptive, where it doesn't take a stand but just establishes details. Or it can be a strong part of the narrative within the story and contain events that drive the story forward. A sequence can occur in linear time, which is the real time in which events occur, or in non-linear time, when it can cut back and forth between different moments in time.

Documentary sequences, for the most part, are observational. This means that they observe events as they happen. If the film didn't record the event, it would still take place.

For example, a village farmer herding his cattle to graze in the fields is an event that would occur everyday, whether or not there was a sequence that contained it. However, sequences can also be organized. These days, many filmmakers choose to construct or initiate events that can be then included in a sequence. For example, if the film dealt with the issue of the fur trade and how animal rights activists are combating this evil, the filmmaker could organize a rally with a group of activists and use that sequence in the film.

The rally would be a real event and the filmmaker's involvement in organizing it doesn't affect its authenticity.

- ***The Montage***

  A montage is a sequence of sorts. It's a process of combining a number of small shots and weaving them together to communicate a large amount of information in a short time. The shots are usually not strictly continuous in nature nor need they be compiled according to subject. A montage can create a whole new meaning out of the two original meanings of adjacent shots just by coupling them together in a flowing, musical way.

  This visual technique is often used extensively by filmmakers to cover either broad areas of subject matter or to portray emotion. For example, a documentary may use a montage to portray the past life of an individual character in the film, covering large chunks of childhood, adolescence, young adulthood and middle age, all in a matter of seconds.

- ***Talking heads***

  One of the most common features of a documentary is

talking heads. This includes either interviews of people on camera or people talking directly to the audience on camera or both. Since documentary is non-fiction, the idea of people talking to the camera, or a filmmaker seated behind the camera is an acceptable story-telling/ information giving technique. Often these talking heads are experts, people involved in the stories or people who are directly or indirectly related to the subject matter in some form. For example, a film on forest conservation in the Himalayas may have interviews with officials from the government forest dept, with villagers who live in the forests, with conservation experts, people involved with logging and maybe even people protesting against logging.

- ***Colours, textures and Lines***

  Elements of line, texture and colour all carry their own weights in a film, counteracting, reinforcing, counter pointing and balancing each other within frames in a complex system. These are read by the senses of the audience on a sub-conscious level and are used extensively by filmmakers to add new dimensions in film.

  With the advent of multi-coloured films, a whole new visual world opened up to both the audience, who could now see images as they existed in real life, and for filmmakers, who could experiment that much further with the medium. Colour and its presence or absence from a film can make a significant difference to the film's message and mood.

  Colour Symbolism is when colour is used deliberately as a symbol on film. Colour speaks and the language of colour, harnessed in a film, is a powerful one. The choice of hues for certain items or its use in out-of-the-ordinary contexts and even the type of lighting used portrays subliminal messages to the audience.

  A red t-shirt worn by the subject during a sequence may

subliminally portray him as a passionate person to the audience. Background colours or the time of day (an orange sunset or an over-exposed, sunny afternoon) have their own symbolism. A dark silhouette of a person walking in an alley may imply he is up to no good.

If a sequence is being organized by the filmmaker, the scriptwriter can have more of a free hand with colour. Demonstrators wearing the colours of a funeral may be protesting the death of democracy; Bright, kitsch clothing may, on the other hand, represent a generation breaking away from tradition.

Streets filled with different colours may present a vibrant society, a cultural hub, festivity, growth; the same streets in dull grey or faded colours may present poverty, disease and degeneration.

It is important, however, not to get carried away with colour. That is where **Colour Pertinence** comes in. There are millions of hues to choose from and vast possibilities when using colour to communicate with the audience. It is easy to get carried away and try and use colour excessively as a medium. Documentaries are about authenticity and the scriptwriter must always remember that subject comes before form.

The elements the scriptwriter uses must be in keeping with real events and people. Also, colour can be a powerful element when it is used with discretion and subtlety. Too much colour may give irritate the audience's senses or may confuse them. Too many colours may lead to the audience overlooking their individual significance or misunderstanding the message.

Textures within a film work on very much the same principles as colour. Texture is important, not only in terms of the inherent texture of the subject but also the texture of the image. Documentary filmmakers often use texture to their advantage by giving old footage a 'grainy' texture, thereby signifying that the footage is of real events that happened in the past.

A 'sepia' texture is often used in recreations/flashbacks for the same purpose. Layering of different shots on top of each other in a half-dissolve has become a popular technique with documentary filmmakers as it creates an almost musical texture.

Lines and form within a frame in a documentary film are also important and can add another dimension. A man walking tall amidst the vertical columns of an old building will immediately be perceived by the audience as someone powerful.

The same columns bathed in dark lighting so that only the layers are shown may imply that he has a dark or negative power. In the same way, a man lying in a field of short grass and looking at a flat, striking horizon may be perceived as submissive to the grandeur of nature.

In feature films, these elements are used extensively by filmmakers and they can be applied within real environments by documentary filmmakers as well. Even though, in documentaries, there is sometimes little control over the objects and locations to be shot on camera, the scriptwriter can still incorporate them into the story in many ways by suggesting interesting shots and sequences that are pertinent and relevant to the subject matter. However, this level of detail need not be attempted for every shot and every sequence within the script as documentaries naturally tend to involve less image control.

2. Sound Elements

Sound is as important as the image. Unfortunately, this fact wasn't realized until quite recently. Sound has always been an extremely underrated aspect of filmmaking and, consequently, sound syntax and even technology developed quite slowly compared to its visual counterpart.

One of the reasons this may have happened is because the audience does not 'read' sound in the same way that it does the visual image. Sound is not only omnipresent but also omni-directional and this pervasiveness led to it being traditionally discounted as an important medium of film.

These days, the same pervasiveness is considered beneficial and filmmakers have learnt that sound can be manipulated effectively to enhance a film. The fact is, sound is sometimes far more effective a medium in film than the visual image. Christian Metz identified five channels of information in film: (a) the visual image (b) print and other graphics (c) speech (d) music; and (e) noise.

Interestingly, three of the five channels are auditory rather than visual, giving testament to the importance of sound in any film. However, even though it's given its due by filmmakers, fiction and documentary alike, sound is often not considered enough at the scriptwriting stage.

A soundtrack can strengthen script moments and sequences and realize both space and time. In documentary, sound can be a vivid counterpart to the visual, adding to the drama and realism of the overall film. It is for this reason that the scriptwriter must incorporate sound into the script. Normally, there are six types of sound in a film:

1. Narrative commentary / Voice over

Narration is the sound-track commentary that sometimes accompanies a visual image in a documentary. It's also often called a 'voice-over' and it can be spoken by one or more off-screen commentators.

The commentator can be virtually anybody, from a character in the film, the filmmaker to even someone completely unidentified, whom the audience only relates to by his/her voice.

Voice-over narration has always been a very popular tool in documentaries because it is an easy and effective way to communicate verbal information in the absence of dialogue between actors. However, many filmmakers choose to do away with narration, preferring to communicate verbal information to the audience through talking heads.

2. Talking heads

The speech element of talking heads, or interviews, is an important element of the soundtrack and also an effective way to communicate information to the audience. In documentary, filmmakers often choose to discard narration completely in favour of talking heads, as they come across as more credible and in keeping with the non-fiction nature of documentary. The audience is able to identify the person talking, thus making their experience more organic for them.

The filmmaker is then also able to show the interviewee talking, cut to visual images while continuing the voice of the interviewee over these images, which may support or supplement what he is saying. This provides a smooth flow of sound for the audience, who will 'know' the voice they are listening to and thus feel more empathy with it.

Narration and talking heads are not exclusive of each other as audio communication techniques. Even though some filmmakers prefer only using talking heads these days, many documentaries have a bit of both and they work quite well together.

3. Music

Feature films have traditionally always relied heavily on music as part of the soundtrack. Music directors and composers would create masterpieces, which sometimes carried entire visual sequences. Some films were even defined and identified by their trademark musical soundtracks.

It is often said that the musical theme of the feature film *Jaws* (1975) created an entire generation of people afraid to swim in the ocean for fear of a shark attack. Like feature films, documentaries also use music to enhance moments and create moods and cultural flavour in the film. Background music appeals on an emotional level with the audience and increases the level of empathy with the events on screen.

Music is also used to establish a particular geographical location or identify a particular community; for example, images of a rice field, accompanied by Indian folk music, easily identify the location as somewhere in India.

4. Ambiance sound

The sound that is naturally present in the atmosphere surrounding the visual image and is recorded simultaneously with it is called ambiance sound. Traditionally, this sound was referred to as 'noise' and speech and music were given more attention. However, as sound technology developed, filmmakers realized its importance in the construction of a complete soundtrack. More than anything else, this type of sound is essential to the creation of a location atmosphere.

The environment's sound or what is often called 'room tone', based on the reverberation time and harmonics of a particular location is its signature.

In documentary, ambiance sound is a necessary part of the soundtrack as it establishes the film's visual in reality and gives the audience a realization of space and time. This is invaluable when dealing with non-fictional subjects. Normally, ambiance sound is used continuously, along with other types of sound, throughout most of the documentary.

5. Sound effects

Any sound that is not speech, music or ambiance and is artificially injected into the soundtrack to enhance it is called a sound effect. This could be a natural sound like a bird chirping to a digitally created or distorted sound like microphone feedback etc. In the old days of film, sound technicians would have to create thousands of sound effects to put in a film in the absence of ambiance sound. This was needed when either the camera was unable to record sound or when shooting took place in studios, where the ambiance would have been at odds with the visuals on screen.

These days, sound effects are used to enhance the film's subject or mood, during recreations or when the required sound is missing from the recorded ambiance.

For example: sounds of horses galloping, men screaming and the clang of weapons against each other could be used while showing a recreated sequence of an ancient battle; or the sound of a helicopter could be injected into a shot of a helicopter flying that was shot from too far away to catch the original ambiance.

6. Silence

It may sound odd to add the lack of sound as a type of sound element, but in the world of film, where everything is deliberate, even silence within the film means that the filmmaker has chosen to put it there.

In the days of silent films, filmmakers used to hire live orchestras to play while thc film was being screened to add to their entertainment value. Today's filmmakers have realized the power of silence. The lack of any sound over a particular moment in a film forces the audience to focus on the visual and heightens their anticipation for the moment when the something happens or when sound re-enters the picture.

This is a technique used quite frequently in horror films. In documentary, the scriptwriter can use this technique when he wants the audience to hone in on the visual to such an extent that it takes them into a kind of suspended or unnatural reality. However, unless it is a silent film or silence plays a thematic role in the film, this element should be used sparingly. Too long a gap between sounds will struggle to hold audience attention.

3. Story Elements

Music, whether it's hip-hop or classical, would just be noise without a story. A painting would be just a collage without a story. Across art forms, the innate story is as variable as it is constant.

A script is not just a compilation of words. It is a compilation of conceptual elements that tell a story. These elements when woven together with audiovisual elements create a good film.

Every film, fiction or documentary, tells a story. The elements of story have been borrowed over time from other art forms like literature and theatre and adapted to suit film form. The story and its structure are often what make the difference between a good script and an average one and it is important for any scriptwriter to study them thoroughly.

Like in all other art forms, film story has three broad structural elements:

- **A beginning**
- **A middle**
- **An end**

The beginning

The importance of a good beginning cannot be stressed enough. The beginning sets the audience up for all the events about to occur in the film. It sets the tone and mood for the film and hints at surprises that lie ahead by raising the right questions in the minds of the audience. In documentary, the beginning always addresses the issue at hand and introduces the subject to the audience.

A good beginning does these things:

1. **Creates an audiovisual 'hook'** to catch the

audience's interest. A 'hook' is something that demands attention and places the film contextually in space and time. It sets up the flavour of things to come, both in a story and audiovisual sense.

2. Establishes the 'core assertion' of the film, which is the point the filmmaker wants to make through the documentary and the message he wants to communicate to the audience. It is this message around which the entire film is built going forward.

3. Creates curiosity among the audience. A good beginning reveals the subject and issue at hand to the audience in such a way that they become keen to see the events that follow in the film.

4. Shows change or the promise of change, which is one of the inherent elements of story and of film.

5. Creates the element of consequence, which is one event leading to another. Cause and effect will direct the audience and increase their understanding of the subject matter.

The Inciting Incident is often a common feature used in the beginning to start a story. It is an incident that radically upsets the balance of forces within the film's story. It is a dynamic and fully developed event, not something vague. As a story begins, the forces at play arc arranged in a particular way, whether they are balanced or not. The inciting incident is any event that swings reality in either a negative or positive way, creating imbalance relative to the previous way.

This storytelling technique is useful because the forces within the film must then react to the inciting incident, setting the story on its way into the middle. For example; the leader of a small desert community could be informed that a large corporation was planning to buy the nearest oasis from the government, effectively creating a water crunch in his community. The leader could be spurred to then organize his people to ensure the government doesn't sell their precious natural water supply.

The leader obtaining the knowledge that his community's water supply was in trouble is the inciting incident. This incident upset the balance of forces and impelled them to react.

The Middle

The big, unwritten space that is the middle of the film is often a daunting challenge for the scriptwriter. Many scriptwriters focus on the dramatic beginning and end of their film and get confused and lost in the middle, leading to a meandering series of events that lack focus.

The key to a good middle is structure. The scriptwriter must ensure that the middle of the film presents a chain of logic designed to prove its core assertion. Each event and action must be pertinent and in keeping with the subject and tone of the film. The issues at hand must be kept in strict focus and events must be arranged in such a way to ensure that the film keeps moving along and progressing. This 'tight' structure will result in a dynamic and interesting middle.

In order to ensure an effective middle, it helps to divide it further into independent parts, which come together to form a whole and tell the story. Thereby, the scriptwriter can think in terms of small, contained chunks of information and place them according to relevance and importance. These chunks of information are sequences.

A good middle consists of good sequences, which also have their own beginnings, middles and ends. Within the sequences, the flow of events determines these parameters. There could many types of sequences within a film, ranging from the dramatic ones that decide the film's direction, to the sequences that lead up to and follow after the dramatic ones. The scriptwriter must allot a particular message for each sequence and ensure that each one has an impact on its own. Then, he can explore the order in which he will place them all depending on flow of information and the gradual increase of impact.

These sequences must be related to each other and unified as a whole in order to give the film a flow. The scriptwriter can use the following criteria to relate and unify them:

1. Concept, idea, thought – The most common link between sequences is subject matter. Each sequence is related with the others through the common issues it deals with.

2. Action – Sequences can be related to each other through the kinds of events and actions they portray.

3. Setting – Many of the sequences may share a common location and many more may have different locations within a common, larger setting.

4. Character – Sequences in a film often share the same characters and are, therefore, unified by these common characters.

5. Mood – Sequences can often relate to each other by having a common flavour or mood. For example, one sequence could show slum streets around the world, another could show the defeated faces of employment seekers. The two sequences are related by the gravity and desolation of their mood.

The Elements of Pacing - Rhythm and Tempo

Because a story is a metaphor of life, we expect it to feel like life, to have the pace, rhythm and tempo of life. *Rhythm* is set by the length of sequences. It is important to vary the length of sequences and not keep them long or repetitive.

Most sequences are visually expressive in one location within two or three minutes. A sequence held too long in one place becomes redundant and loses audience attention. *Tempo* is the level of activity within a sequence. A person staring out of a window contemplating life may have a low tempo; a riot will naturally have a high tempo. In a well-told story, the progression of sequences normally accelerates pace.

As he heads toward a dramatic point in the film, the scriptwriter could take advantage of rhythm and tempo to progressively shorten scenes while the actions in them become more and more brisk. Immediately after a dramatic point in the film, the scriptwriter can 'let the audience breathe' and slow down the pace. Dramatic sequences themselves are usually played out for maximum impact and the length depends very much on the subjects and events of the individual sequence. Pace begins in the script and it is important that the scriptwriter to incorporate it at this stage.

'Beats'

Beats are a useful technique often used by scriptwriters in creating pace for the film. A beat is the smallest element of structural technique

It is an exchange of behavior in action/reaction. Beat by beat these changing behaviors shape a sequence. A sequence needn't be built up of just one action. It can have multiple actions, and each action is one beat. For example; A man could walk into a room, walk to the window and look out, sit down on a chair, pick up a book and read it, put down the book, get up and leave the room. This sequence has five beats – 1. Walking into the room, 2. Looking out the window, 3. Sitting down, 4. Reading a book 5. Getting up and out of the room.

The scriptwriter can benefit from breaking down each sequence into beats because he can then have greater control over the sequence. He can shave off beats to make a sequence shorter, add more beats to make it longer or increase and decrease the tempo of beats to suit the point of time in which the sequence occurs. In documentary, the scriptwriter may have limited control over the nature of actions that take place in a sequence, but he can control how many of them feature in the final film.

Linear Vs Non-linear time

The scriptwriter also has a choice whether to order the sequences in linear time, meaning a temporal order of the events that occurred, or in non-linear time, a random order where the film can switch back and forth between events that occurred at different points of time without any temporal continuity.

Whereas linear time is a more traditional method of arranging sequences, many documentary scriptwriters these days opt for non-linear time to tell a story. Nonlinear time is generally held to the more 'interesting' of the two because the scriptwriter has far greater control over the amount of information revealed to the audience at every stage since they may not initially follow the order of events.

However, this is a difficult arrangement to master and the scriptwriter needs to be completely clued into the audience reactions and provide information in a succinct manner so as not to confuse or overwhelm them.

The scriptwriter can also combine the two arrangements to the extent that he can have some sequences arranged chronologically and occasionally slip into the future or the past using flashbacks and recreations.

Transitions

Every story needs to have a seamless progression between sequences for the entire thing to work. For this, it needs to have something to link the tail of each sequence to the head of the next sequence. Generally, we find this linking element in one of two possibilities: what the two sequences have in common, or what they have in opposition. A 'Transition' is something held in common by two sequences or counter pointed between them. This common or counter element can be many different things:

- ***A character trait or situation***; Two adjacent sequences could feature people with similar or completely opposite traits and the transition would be smooth. For example;

the eyes of a man to the eyes of a woman, or the eyes of a man who can see to the eyes of a blind man.

• ***An action***; Any event that continues naturally from one to the other has a smooth transition, as do events that may follow each other chronologically, but are opposites. For example, boisterous noise in a room to cold silence.

• ***An object***; A smooth transition would be between two similar objects, like a greenhouse interior to a forest, or two opposites, like the Sahara Desert to the Arctic.

• ***A word***; a word or a phrase used in the narrative could link two sequences. For example, the same word occurring in both sequences or one sequence featuring the word 'dark' and the next featuring the word 'light' in the narrative.

• ***A quality of light***; two similar or opposite moods created by film lighting could transition sequences smoothly. For example; a shadowy meadow to a shadowy room or a bright afternoon to a clear, moonlight night.

• ***A sound***; one sound or similar type of sound could be a 'soundbridge' between two sequences, or one type of sound could turn into its exact opposite. For example, the notes of a violin from one violin player to an orchestra or from the notes of a violin to the din of construction machinery.

• ***An idea***; an abstract idea, metaphor or concept could connect two sequences as well. For example, a wilting bunch of flowers to the deathbed of an old man.

The Element of Progression

Many a time, a film starts off with a bang and fizzles down to a boring rut by the time it reaches the middle. This is the result of the scriptwriter's imagination going limp at the worst possible time. The scriptwriter must keep in mind that a story must not retreat to actions of lesser intensity or magnitude but move progressively forward to a final action.

The events must become bigger and better and their excitement and involvement must gradually increase as the film move forward. This is called progression. The scriptwriter must never resort to repetition, staying on one point too long or showing too many similar events.

The movement forward needs to be sharp and planned. This presents a tricky problem to the scriptwriter in terms of how to express the element of progression. Broadly, there are four techniques to this:

- **Social Progression** – this is when the film progressively widens its character's actions and expressions into society and social situations. Gradually, the film may feature more and more people, allow their actions to ramify outward into their communities and into the world around them thereby affecting the lives of other people.

  The idea behind this technique is to start small with only a few people and a simpler story, then gradually build and add more dimensions to it in a powerful progression of events. For example; a story about a farmer's land being repossessed by the government could lead to the documentary questioning government policy and involving farmers from all over the country.

- **Personal Progression** – If the subject matter of the film doesn't require an outward progression, then it can be just as effective to progress inwards instead. Human beings are deeper within than has been discovered and there is plenty of material inside our minds and hearts for a documentary to explore. The idea behind this technique is to start with a simple storyline and go from the outside in, making it more and more layered emotionally, psychologically, physically, morally and perhaps even go into darker elements of the human personality.

  For example; a story about a man struggling to deal with

survivor's guilt could go deep into human psychology and explore how we perceive death and dealing with surviving a deadly situation while another didn't make it.

- **Symbolic ascension** – There are countless, imaginative realms of symbolism to which a film could progress. The scriptwriter could build the symbolic energy of the story from the particular to the universal, from the specific to the archetypal. Subliminal symbolism, added subtly to a film in layers lifts the telling of a story into the next level of expression. As the story progresses, the film could feature concepts and images that are more and more meaningful until everything stands for universal ideas.

  This technique may not be completely in keeping with the realism of documentary, but it can be used extensively if the subject is in keeping with the symbolic nature of the film. For example; a film on art could progress from a painter's story to symbolic expressions of art and the universal need for artistic expression.

- **Ironic ascension** – Irony is not a straightforward concept. It sees life in duality and plays with our ideas of what seems and what is. To portray irony with words is easier than in a story on film. The scriptwriter needs to have an ironic sense to incorporate it into a film with élan. He must also put a lot of trust in the audience's ability to 'get' the irony.

A film with ironic ascension could show a progressively dominant play between actions and results and between appearance and reality. For example; a documentary could feature a community fighting for their right to information and for the government to release confidential local documents. They could, as the film progresses, discover that they could gain the right to access confidential documents, but most had already been destroyed.

The End

In the words of Aristotle, an ending must be both 'inevitable' and 'unexpected.' The end of a film is what the audience takes home with them. It is the primary factor that determines audience opinion about the film they've just seen.

The end is when the film concludes with a conclusion, usually a reiteration of the core assertion of the film. In many films, this is done by hammering home the assertion with a 'key feature', which could be a anything from a phrase to a visual, or many visuals, to one last event that sets the impression to be left on the audience in stone. All or many issues are hopefully, or at least temporarily, resolved in the end of a film. That is why it is also called the Resolution of the film.

Broadly speaking, there are two types of film endings in documentary:

- **Closed End**

  A closed ending is usually one where all the questions raised in the story are answered and all emotions evoked are satisfied. The audience is left with a rounded and closed, overall experience that leaves nothing further to doubt or question.

  This type of ending is absolute and irreversible and the film's subject cannot be extended. For example; a documentary about a particular sect of women working to change divorce law by passing a bill in parliament could end with the bill being passed and the battle being won. This kind of ending doesn't leave anything further to be said on the matter and the audience is left with a feeling of closure.

- **Open End**

  An open ending is usually one which leaves one, some or many questions unanswered and some emotions unfulfilled. This type of ending relies heavily on audience imagination to fill in the gaps once the lights have come on.

  The 'open' implication doesn't mean the film finishes in

the middle, leaving everything hanging unresolved. The questions left are answerable and the emotions resolvable and all that has gone before has led to clear and limited alternatives that make a certain degree of closure possible for the audience.

For example; a documentary about interreligious relations during Independence Day celebrations in a particular country may end as night falls on the festivities, but many questions as to the future of relations between the religious groups may be left unanswered.

This type of ending has become very popular in documentary films after many filmmakers started realizing that the issues most documentaries deal with are part of larger problems facing the world to which there are no clear cut solutions or answers.

Each ending has a decided flavour, a mood. A resolution can occur in so many different ways. 'Happy endings' have always been popular in feature films as they leave the audience on a 'happy high.' In documentary, things are not so straightforward. The flavour or mood of the ending must be determined by the events of real life and cannot be controlled by the scriptwriter.

Depending on the events that occur, the ending can be optimistic, pessimistic or even ironic in nature.

The scriptwriter must judge the mood of the ending after studying the conclusions the film has come to based on the turn of events. Some issues may be left unresolved, some may have taken a turn for the worse. Many scriptwriters feel the pressure to 'find the silver lining' and leave the audience on a high, but they should be obliged to stick to the truth and tell it like it is.

The end of a feature film is often called a 'climax'. It is when the story builds to a last revolution in values from positive to negative or negative to positive, with or without irony, at maximum charge that's absolute and irreversible. Basically, something big happens in the end that changes the film radically and moves the audience.

The process of building to this climactic end is also often applied to documentaries in a toned down manner because it works so well in feature films.

'Saving the best for last' is the old adage and the climactic sequence/series of sequences are the most meaningful and dramatic in the film in terms of resolving the issues at hand.

The climax is the last leap of the scriptwriter's imagination and should be clear and self-evident, requiring no explanation and playing out in a dramatic rhythm and tempo. For example; a documentary about two boxing champions may end with a climactic series of sequences in which they fight each other for the boxing title.

The scriptwriter could make winning or losing the title into a spectacular drama played out in the ring and keep the audience on the edge of their seats.

Character

Traditionally, characters were the people in the film. However, as both fiction and documentary films became more varied and complex, this simplistic view of who or what is a character was discarded and a new definition was coined based on a broader scope. Simply put, characters are the significant 'beings' in your film. A character can be human, animal and, in some films, even an object or a location. Anything that has the ability to take action or suffer consequences can be a character.

However, a character is always viewed from a human perspective. This is just simply because the filmmakers are human and the audience is human and therefore, we unconsciously try and attribute human qualities to all characters in a film, even though they may not be human.

For a scriptwriter, it helps to think of characters from this angle as it makes them more understandable. People are easier to deal with than, say, a rock. As humans, we may never understand a rock completely, so we can portray it as a character in a film with regards to its relationship with humans. When studying characters, it always helps to go back to the traditional definition and think of them as human, the people in a film.

Character is a central part of story structure and is regarded as possibly the most important aspect of a film by many. Every film must have characters and whatever happens within a film, must happen to the characters.

They are our representatives inside the film, experiencing it for us, making complex topics accessible to us as viewers. If the story is about people, then the people the story is about are the characters. If the story and subject is not about people then the people the story affects are the characters.

For example; if the documentary is about a married couple and the process of them getting a divorce, then the characters in the film are the couple themselves and the people facilitating or opposing the divorce like family members, lawyers etc.

If the film is about democracy, then the characters in the film could be representatives among a larger population whom democracy, or the lack of it, affects. These could be citizens of a country, policy makers or perhaps members of government institutions and the press.

There are two broad types of characters in a film:

- **Central character/s**

  The character the story is about is a central character. This is the protagonist whose story is being told in the film. It could be one person or a few people. These people are directly related to the subject at hand and are the primary vehicles that carry the story forward through their actions and reactions.

- **Secondary character/s**

  The characters that surround the central character are

the secondary characters. These characters are usually indirectly related to the subject at hand and are playing a part in helping the central character proceed in the story. The story is not about them, they are part of the larger story. These characters interact indirectly with the story through the central character.

Single Protagonist Vs Multiple Central Characters

A film about a school boy who faces bulling in school has one central character – the boy himself. A film about a group of four school children who have been victims of bullying and have come together to stop this practice in their school may have the four children as central characters unless the scriptwriter chooses to tell the story through only one of the children, thereby making him the central character.

The decision to tell a story through one protagonist or multiple protagonists depends on a few factors like the scope of the subject and whether it needs more characters to cover that scope, the types of people involved in the story and to what extent they are a part of it and the length of the film and how many characters can realistically be featured during that time. A single protagonist may result in a focused, simpler film and will also be easier to tackle in terms of story.

However, multiple protagonists, while making a story more complex and difficult to write, may add variety, multiple dimensions and interest to the film. It is not advisable, however, to have too many protagonists in one film as the audience will get confused after a point. Many multiple characters make a story more horizontal, spreading it out in scope, and this may hinder the vertical progression of the film after a point.

True Character and Characterisation

Characters have personalities. In fiction films, characters are created by the scriptwriter and are fictional representations of real people. In documentary films, characters actually are real people with real traits. While the scriptwriter may not have control over the kind of personality traits the characters in his film have, it is imperative that he study these traits and incorporate them in the script. *Characterisation* is a writer's term for the sum of all the visible traits of a character in the film. Age, gender and IQ, speech and gesture, education and occupation, personality, values and attitudes. The totality of various combinations of these traits makes each person unique. A character may be an ambitious, confident woman, who has a good sense of humour and loves sports.

She may be impatient and demanding of others around her and have a chip on her shoulder about being a woman in a man's world. She may have feminist beliefs but loves cooking and cleaning. These traits are visible parts of her personality and can be incorporated easily by the scriptwriter into the woman's actions in the film. These traits are also important in making the audience 'connect' with the woman on a human level. She is like them, shares parts of their own personalities and, therefore, they can relate to her.

True character is revealed in the choices a character makes under pressure – the greater the pressure, the deeper the revelation, the truer the choice to the character's essential nature. True character lies beneath characterization and is revealed slowly to the audience over the course of the film through the actions of the character. It asks the question, 'Regardless of appearances, who really is this person?' Is the woman courageous or cowardly, generous or selfish? As she chooses, she is. For example, the same woman, despite believing herself to be a compassionate person, may witness an accident on the road in the middle of the night and not stop to help the victims for fear of her own safety. By her choice, she has revealed an aspect of her true character to the audience. This is an important aspect of character and should be studied and incorporated by the scriptwriter into the documentary as far as possible. The gradual revelation of true character adds incredible dimension, surprise and audience interest in a film.

The 'Plot' of the Story

The words 'to plot' literally means to figure out a path to enter or exit a situation. In a story sense 'the plot' is when a story navigates through branching possibilities to choose a path that will lead to a resolution. The plot of a story is where every sequence in the film makes the next one inevitable because of their events and design in time. Every story needs to have a plot, no matter how small, to move the story forward towards a goal. There needn't be dramatic twists and turns or high pressure suspense or shocking surprise. A plot can merely be a selection of events and their patterns displayed through time in the film. The scriptwriter must make event choices – what to include and what to exclude – and place them in a particular order.

The plot is a unifying force that holds a story together. If the film were a human body, then the plot would be the spine, creating unity between all the elements. Even when the story portrays chaos, the plot is what keeps the audience on track. The plot always adheres to a 'controlling idea', which is the ultimate point that the film is trying to make.

The plot of the film is designed as a larger whole by the scriptwriter. In many cases, the film starts a plot in one direction and then makes it change direction sometime during a film towards a completely new goal. For example; a documentary film that shows a lawyer trying to defend his young, male client could start off with a strong belief in the innocence of the man. Then, in the middle of the film, the lawyer could be presented with startling evidence that shows his client was guilty and he could actually try and have him convicted. This sweeping change that takes the film from one condition to a changed condition by the end is called the *Plot Arc*.

There are broadly three types of plot:

- **The Archplot** – The Archplot is a classic plot design. It has well-defined characters that face situations outside of themselves. The progression is more social and external and the treatment is set in continuous, linear time. The Archplot has a strong sense of reality and there is a closed ending. The plot arc has absolute, irreversible change.

- **The Miniplot** – The Mini-plot is a minimalist form of archplot. It features trimmed, simpler elements with less fuss over the details. There is an economy of both design and treatment and audiovisual rules along with the rules of story are less rigidly followed. The elements of a miniplot can include internal or personal progression, an open ending and multiple protagonists.

- **The Antiplot** – The Anti-plot reverses everything classical and contradicts most of the traditional elements of story and structure. The idea perhaps is to ridicule the very idea of formal principles. Although uncommon so far in documentaries, films with anti-plot are becoming more popular. These kinds of films tend to be ambitious, revolutionary and even extravagant. Their elements often include coincidence, nonlinear time and inconsistent realities.

Many films also have *Subplots*. These are smaller plots that make up different, simultaneous and, often contradictory, parts of a larger plot. Subplots are self-contained stories that adhere to the controlling idea of the film but also add a new, related dimension to the film. Most documentaries have one or more subplots as they often tend to deal with issues that are tied in with other issues. Subplots don't take away but rather add to the main plot and their individual beginnings, middles and ends take place in the middle of the main plot.

The resolutions of subplots help drive the main plot to its own resolution. The scriptwriter can use this technique to include different ideas and events that are related to but not directly part of the main storyline. For example; a film about an adopted girl's search for her birth mother could also feature a subplot about another girl who found her birth mother and wished she hadn't started looking in the first place. This subplot then raises doubts as to whether the main character's meeting with her own birth mother would be a happy or sad one.

The 'Backstory'

Simply put, the backstory is the background story that occurred before the start of the film. For example; a film about a farmer trying to stop a bank from repossessing his farmland could very well start with the farmer having a conversation with a lawyer. The backstory in this film would be that the farmer was going about his work but having trouble repaying his debts to the bank when, one day, he was given a repossession notice and asked to vacate. The backstory is crucial in providing the audience with some context for the story and the scriptwriter must provide them with this information at some stage, either visually or verbally, in the narrative. A few ways of doing this are having characters talk about what happened previously, show it visually through a dramatized recreation of events or through records of events like newspaper clippings etc.

Point of View/POV

Each story is set in a specific time and place, yet sequence by sequence, as the audience look at events happening on screen, where do they locate themselves in space to view the action? This is point of view – the angle taken to look at the events and characters, their interactions with each other and the environment in the film. The scriptwriter's choice of point of view or POV makes an enormous difference on how the audience views the film. This is because who or whatever's POV is shown is the person/thing that is telling the story to the audience.

A story is told in many different ways – through visuals, sound, words, characters, events etc. However, the scriptwriter must make the decision early on as to who will tell the story to the audience. This decision then binds the story to the limited experience of that entity. Suppose a number of people had a shared experience like a plane crash. Each person on the plane had a different experience and different POV so each one would have a different story to tell.

One of them couldn't tell you anything about another's experience. So, as a scriptwriter, if you wanted to show this event on film, you would need to narrow down on one or a few of the passengers and only show the event through their eyes. It would be possible to hopscotch through time and space, picking up bits and pieces of everyone's experience, but this would probably make the story sprawl and become unfocused.

The way in which the scriptwriter chooses to tell the story through focused POV is called a *Narrative*. This literally means someone or something is narrating the story. Narrative is different from Narration, which is restricted to the spoken word. Narrative is a combination of audiovisual elements, story elements and is when a particular entity's POV uses the various elements to tell the story. In other words, POV gives or drives the narrative. Once the POV of a sequence has been decided, then the shots are taken from that POV, the sound is tailored towards it and the information given to the audience is limited by it.

- ***First-person POV***

  This is one of the most common types of POV used in documentary. It is the direct POV of one or more characters in the film. They talk in terms of 'I' and the narrative is done through their eyes and records their experiences. In this type of POV, the character can either be featured on screen in an interview, perform actions or be part of events on screen and/or his voice can be featured as part of the sound track while the visuals can relate to what he is saying. For example; a film about a boy who ran the marathon could feature him narrating the story. The visual structure would be from his POV, the events would be limited to his experience of them as would his story.

Sometimes, a film switches between different POVs of characters in a film to get a more rounded view of events and give the audience a wider perspective. Each person whose POV drives the narrative is then allotted sequences of their own and the scriptwriter must tailor these sequences to comply with that particular character's limited POV. This way the audience may experience the film from different POVs but is still only experiencing them one at a time.

• ***Second-Person POV***

This kind of POV, where the narrative of the film directly addresses the audience as 'you' and forces the audience into the story is less common in documentaries and more a feature of television video magazines and news stories.

• ***Third Person POV***

This kind of POV is much more common in more classical documentaries. It is a narrative told from the POV of someone unknown to the audience, a god-like omnipresent person who see events from all sides and can read the inner worlds of characters. This person is never identified by the film, but usually the soundtrack features this person's voice talking about the characters directly to the audience in terms of 'he' or 'she'. This person knows everything about everyone and therefore the narrative is from a general perspective, as if the camera itself is this person. This kind of POV gives the audience a less direct view of the story, since the characters aren't dispensing information themselves, but it also allows the audience to have a much fuller experience of the story.

Sometimes, films combine first and third-person POVs and have an overall thirdperson POV while switching to talking heads with the characters during the film. However, while this gives the characters a voice in the film, their own part in the narrative is only as characters and not as narrators.

◆ ◆ ◆

6

PUTTING A SCRIPT TOGETHER

As difficult as it seems, combining visual, audio and story elements into a documentary script, at its most basic level, can be as simple as following a few scriptwriting tips and techniques that have been known to work in many films.

The Three Sacred 'C's

- **Character**

Everyone knows films have characters. But why? In a film about democracy, for example, what is the need for characters when the subject of the film is an idea? The answer is simple; characters give a human face to any story. They experience the story for the audience watching the film. Even if the subject of the film doesn't involve people, most films will show characters within the subject to 'humanise' the film and make it more accessible. That said, in a film about an idea like democracy, it wouldn't make sense to include characters that are not directly or indirectly related to the subject matter.

For instance, a woman experiencing having a baby is not really connected in any way to democracy, so it wouldn't make sense for her to be in the film. Not unless she was a reporter who was talking about freedom of the press and there was very little of her pregnancy covered in her film experiences.

There is also a reason for the scriptwriter to study characterization and true character carefully and represent both in the character's actions on film. The more the audience knows about a person in the film, the closer they feel to that person. This empathy is important to create because, through it, the audience can get emotionally involved in the film and be that much more affected by it when the lights come on. They start to 'root' for a character they empathize with because the have unconsciously put themselves in the character's place and are imagining having the same experiences.

This audience-character bond will have the audience laughing and crying with the character throughout the film, especially in a documentary, where they realize that the character is real and so are the events.

Characters can often identified by the nature of their actions, or lack of them. *Active Characters* are those that initiate the events that take place around them. They take action and make things happen. For example; a character who decides that a particular law is detrimental to society and starts a campaign to change the law is an active character. *Passive Characters*, on the other hand, react to situations thrust upon them without any choosing of their own.

Their actions are brought upon by things happening to them. For example; a farmer whose village has seen drought for 2 years may struggle to make ends meet is a passive character.

Sometimes, the filmmaker himself chooses to become a character in his film. In this way, he can directly experience the story for himself and his narrative can be a much more personal one. The point in time that the filmmaker enters the film is called 'the point of attack.'

This narrative works very well when the characters in the film are culturally and socially different from the audience, who may have trouble seeing things from their point of view. The filmmaker as a main character can then bridge that gap between the audience and the characters.

- **Conflict**

Conflict is one of the most important aspects of a film, documentary or fiction. To put it simply, conflict is to film what sound is to music. Without it, all the elements of a film are useless because there is no reason for them to move forward. When the main character/s step into the inciting incident, they enter a world governed by conflict and when conflict ends, the film ends. The most difficult task of a film is to hold audience interest and attention and carry them through time without an awareness of it. Conflict has till date been the only thing able to do that perhaps because the audience themselves experience conflict in many forms every day of their lives and a life without conflict would seem abnormal and boring. Since conflict is, whether we like it or not, such an integral part of life and film replicates life, conflict becomes indispensable in film.

So who goes through conflict? The characters do. The try and attain their goals in the face of opposition and obstacles. These opposing forces could be big or small, one or many, brief or protracted and in any shape or form.

Opposition could come from other characters with incompatible goals, organized entities or the situation and environment surrounding the characters. The characters struggling in the face of conflict, even if the amount of struggle is as miniscule as walking with a stone in your shoe, make the story move ahead.

In fiction films, the scriptwriter creates conflict in imaginary situations with imaginary characters. In documentary, the scriptwriter has to study the various conflicts facing the story's real life characters and portray them in the film. He must then follow the characters as they try and overcome their 'opponents' in the story.

The Principle of Antagonism is a good measure of conflict. It states that a protagonist and his story can only be as intellectually fascinating and emotionally compelling to the audience as the forces of antagonism make them. This is not to say the more the conflict the better the film. Instead, the more developed the antagonism or conflict facing the characters, the more they realize the story by facing them.

They face a journey that helps them realize themselves as well. For example; a documentary film about first-year college students learning to live by themselves and being away from home may feature its main characters facing the challenges that come with living alone for the first time, like overcoming loneliness, keeping a house, studying hard etc. At the end of their first-year, they would be different people who realized new aspects of their personalities.

Without the challenges, they would have just been college students living uncomplicated lives and the story would have lacked interest.

There are generally two types of conflict that characters in a film must face. The first is Outer Conflict. They must face antagonism outside of themselves from the world around them. This could be from other people, objects, organizations or the environment. The second type is Inner Conflict. The characters must face conflict inside of themselves.

This may include their psychology, weaknesses, fears, dark sides etc. It involves the inner world of the character's minds. Many films have a combination of both types because, as with real life, one rarely occurs with the exclusion of the other.

In documentary, it should obviously not be taken for

granted that the character overcomes all or any of the conflict. Real life isn't always made up of heroes and villains and the character may fail to achieve what he set out to do.

- **Change**

An audience watches a film with the desire to 'see what happens.' Therefore, something, or many things, must definitely happen to keep the audience in their seats. This something is change. Change is some aspect of reality becoming different in a particular way. It is at the root of everything in the world – it is what happens, has happened and will happen. Change is also an extremely intriguing thing for humans because it almost always has consequences, which affect our lives directly or indirectly.

There is no question that change must occur in a film. In the beginning, the inciting incident introduces change to the character's life. In the middle, the character must face conflict and, when he does, things change around him and he changes as well. In the end, something must have changed from the beginning and this change lead to the resolution. The scriptwriter must choose which change to include in the film based on how meaningful the change is. If it is not meaningful, then it doesn't complete the story.

For example; a character could have learnt many things from the experience of trying to cook for the first time, the first being that he learnt how to cook a little better. He learnt from his mistakes and won't make them again, thereby changing him as a person. This is meaningful change. It is the job of the scriptwriter to decide which change is meaningful and incorporate it into the script.

Change naturally moves the story forward. Situation A changes to Situation B, which then changes to Situation C. The story moves forward in this way.

Change can be small or big. Sometimes small changes can happen within or facilitate bigger change. In a documentary, the scriptwriter must study all the various changes that took or are taking place in a character's journey through conflict and decide how to formulate them in a story that is structured and meaningful.

> There are, broadly, two types of change. The first is *Outer Change*. This is when the world around the character changes. This could be physical change, change in other people, objects, situations or the environment.
>
> The second is *Inner Change*. This is when the character himself changes within. This could be his opinions, beliefs, values, personality, psychology or mental or emotional state. When the character changes in a significant manner through the course of the film, it's called the *Character Arc*.

When the audience expects to see change, they naturally expect it to be irreversible. However, sometimes change can reverse back to the way things were before the change took place.

This is in itself a new change even though the film goes back to a previous state. In documentary, as in real life, this often happens and, when it does, the scriptwriter should include it in the script even though nothing really changed in the larger situation. Here, the change itself is what happens.

Writing Visually

Writing visually is not just a question of blindly incorporating visual elements into a film. There are a few important things a scriptwriter must keep in mind:

- ***Show, don't tell*** – The scriptwriter needs to keep in mind that film is a visual medium. Unlike a novel, a film script is never 'read' literally by the audience and therefore the scriptwriter should try and incorporate most of the information he has to give into a visual format. For example; rather than telling the audience that a man is a farmer, the scriptwriter should show the man working in his fields. A potter should be making pottery, a hairdresser cutting someone's hair and so forth. It always helps to show character and event action rather than talk about it or include it in narration because the audience is then able to experience it themselves, making it more real for them. They can also grasp details and take in subconscious information. When given a choice, the scriptwriter must always try and start with a visual image as a base for portrayal of any concept and then use other methods of portrayal only when the visual is not possible.

- ***Show through action and movement*** – There is a reason we call them 'moving images' and the scriptwriter must always try to keep that fact in mind. The visual must be kept moving; the characters must be 'doing' something. The audience will react to movement on screen with interest and to static images with boredom. Wherever possible, the scriptwriter should try and communicate the story to the audience through a moving and action-packed visual narrative.

- ***Visual pertinence*** – Simply put, visual pertinence is keeping the visuals relevant to the subject and sustaining the flow of action. Don't show a farmer working behind a desk in a bank unless he works there part-time. Also, it is important for the scriptwriter to structure sequences according to the point in time they appear in the film. If a character has just suffered a major loss, then don't show a sequence where she goes to a party unless that's what she would do naturally in that situation. The scriptwriter has to place the character's actions in the visuals within the story and make every choice of action, location and image relevant to the story and its subject.

- ***Emotional pertinence*** – When watching a sequence, the audience take in different aspects of it. One of the things an audience receives from a sequence is emotion. The audience naturally reacts to this emotion with their own emotional reaction. Emotional pertinence is controlling the emotional reaction of the audience and making it relevant to the story at that point in the film. This can be done by the scriptwriter by emphasizing emotional details or triggers which will provide the desired emotional response from the audience.

• ***Moods and Metaphors*** – The scriptwriter has many visual tools at his disposal including the control of visual mood and visual metaphors to represent an idea that would be otherwise difficult to portray visually. For example; a sequence which features a man working late into the night in his office could be full of shadows to add to the perception of time. Or, a sequence, which features a man on death row being executed in jail by electric chair, could focus on a light bulb momentarily flickering to signify that the man has died.

• ***Special effects*** – Sometimes, special effects like slow motion, where a visual is slowed down in time, help create and regulate tempo and rhythm in a film as well as enhance emotional value at certain points. Dissolving from one shot to another helps create smoother visual flow. Special effects may or may not be incorporated into the script in great detail. The scriptwriter should only include the specific effects he feels are required to tell the story and are relevant to the subject and mood of the sequence. It is not advisable, however, to use an excess of special effects in a documentary for the simple reason that they alter the nature of reality. This altered reality goes against the very nature of documentary and may or may not be accepted by the audience if it is overdone.

Writing Narration/commentary

An important point for the scriptwriter to remember is that, as crucial as sound is to films, the visual always comes first. Narration, therefore, is secondary to visual. It is a part of the overall narrative, but does not lead the narrative. Therefore, the scriptwriter, even though he is a writer and his first relationship is with words, should not necessarily give the narration a dominant role in the narrative.

The most important decision the scriptwriter has to make concerning narration is deciding who will be the narrator/s. This choice has to be made both on a narrative-relevance level and an artistic level. The narrator needs to be someone who adds value to the film and drives the film's narrative forward. The scriptwriter has the following options in narration:

- **First-person narration**

  A first-person *narration* backs up a first-person *narrative*, where the person whose point of view is currently being represented visually and story-wise is the narrator. This narrator talks in terms of 'I' and brings his limited POV across to the audience via the spoken word. This narrator is a character in the film and he may or may not be shown visually at the time his voice is speaking. When the filmmaker is a character in the film, then the narrator is often the filmmaker himself. First-person narration should follow the rules of first-person narrative, which is that only one character's POV can be shown at a time, despite the fact that multiple characters may be narrators in the film.

- **The 'Voice of God'**

  Third-person narration is often called 'the voice of God' in an unflattering sense. However, it is a popular choice for many documentary films around the world. It is when an all-knowing, omnipresent entity narrates the story, referring to all the characters within the film as 'he' or 'she.' Again, like the third-person narrative, this narrator's POV is all-pervasive even though it is less personal.

Keeping narration visual is normally a challenge for scriptwriters. It is important to remember that narration should back up a visual instead of trying to overpower it. Also, if something is being shown visually, then there is no need for the narration to mention it as well. The narration should say what the visual doesn't say and should be in tune with the actions taking place at that point in the film.

Keeping narration relevant is another challenge. Many scriptwriters use the narration for information-shoving at the audience. The narration should be as focused, clear-cut, short and relevant as possible. Information should be given on a need basis only and when the particular subject has been sufficiently covered, it should stop short of exposition.

Keeping narration simple is the final challenge. Big words and fancy sentences are lost on an audience that has to keep track of multiple elements coming toward them at the same time. In fact, a verbose narration only makes the film harder for them to follow. A good narration is precise and simple and works in tune with the other elements of the film without trying to be grandiose.

A method every scriptwriter must practice is speaking out aloud the words and sentences of the narration as he writes them. This is because the narration will ultimately not be read but spoken and the text has to be of the spoken word. Reading it out aloud with reveal how it sounds and the scriptwriter can correct and replace words or sentences that don't flow. This practice also gives an indication of how much time the narration will take to speak out aloud and will allow him to time the narration according to the length of visual sequences.

Writing Sound

The soundtrack of the film, the music, ambiance and sound effects, can be used by the scriptwriter in two ways within the film script. The first is to make a point on its own, like the sound of a train whistle when the visual only shows a train track, and the second is to reinforce a point that the visual is already making, like sad music when a character is crying with grief. Both are effective ways of incorporating sound at the script stage.

A soundtrack must have Aesthetic Relevance, which is simply relevance to the subject, location and emotion of a particular point in the film. After all, it wouldn't make sense to hear a western music track when showing visuals of rural villages in India or to hear upbeat drums at a particularly sad, slow moment in the film. The scriptwriter should make sure that the soundtrack is always in keeping with the narrative and the audience should hear only a seamless extension of what they see.

In most films, but especially in documentary, the scriptwriter should try and keep a more or less continuous presence of ambiance or natural sound. The ambiance volume may be kept low or high depending on the rest of the soundtrack, but keeping it constant reminds the viewer that the visuals are set in the real world. It is just one more layer that adds to the feeling of authenticity and credibility that documentaries try and establish.

Disclosure

The flow of information in a film is very important, as is the order, amount and frequency with which it is given to the audience. The scriptwriter can use a method called disclosure to control the flow of information. This technique is about withholding as much information as possible until the point when it is absolutely necessary to provide it to the audience. The scriptwriter gives the audience the information in bits and piece, as and when required and never too much at the same time. Then, progressively the bits of information start making sense and adding up to a whole context. The idea behind this technique is to keep the audience guessing and levels of suspense and curiosity high. The scriptwriter can 'bait' the audience with key pieces of information, never too little but never too much, right up until all is revealed.

Idea Vs Counter-idea

A popular technique to create tension and heighten interest in a film is using a debate of ideas. The scriptwriter can forge a story ahead in a dynamic way by moving it back and forth across the opposing charges of its primary value. Simply put, different sequences alternatively express positive and negative dimensions of the controlling idea creating a debate between ideas and counter-ideas within the story. In this way, the scriptwriter can use the element of contradiction as a technique to make the film more vibrant. Eventually, one of these ideas can 'win' and result in a resolution at the end. This technique needn't involve obvious positive and negative elements, like people doing good or bad things in the sequences. There needn't be a value judgment about what is good and bad either. This sequential debate is more to do with the message of each sequence. This message, regardless of the action portrayed in the sequence, has a positive or negative charge and this is what can be played against one another between sequences.

First you 'set up' then you 'pay off'

Another technique often used by scriptwriters is when they set-up layers in knowledge and then pay off by closing the gap and delivering knowledge to the audience. This is done by planting insights or 'visual clues' at various points in the film. These clues are hazy and without context when they are presented to the viewer, who doesn't quite understand them at the time but remembers them because they've been emphasized by the narrative. This is a deliberate move by the scriptwriter. The clue or insight is not meant to make sense on its own. Later on, the scriptwriter provides the larger picture or contextual information in other sequences, closing that gap in knowledge and making the meaning of the clue or insight clear to the audience. By suddenly having the haziness removed, the audience reaction is an 'aha! That's what it meant' and they are intrigued and involved in the story even further.

The scriptwriter's choice

Chances are that there will be many parts of a story that demand representation in a film. The scriptwriter must make a choice about what to include in the film and, more importantly, what to exclude. A gap in the story or missing information and informationoverload are both extremely undesirable situations in a film. The scriptwriter's choice could make the difference between the film making being interesting or not. He must go over the story and narrative with a toothcomb to make sure the sum of all the various parts add up correctly, the flow of information is smooth and relevant and anything excessive or not focused enough is cut out of the film. This is a difficult but necessary decision and the scriptwriter needs to be harsh and let go of bits of the film that he may have grown attached to but just don't make the cut.

A note on Duration

Rarely is a scriptwriter given the privilege of deciding the duration of the film he is writing. This is something predetermined, set by the producer and/or TV channels or others, depending on the film's distribution plan. The scriptwriter has to work within those parameters and tailor the film to suit the desired duration. If, however, a scriptwriter is 'let loose' on the film's duration, then a word of advice; less is usually more. It is better to stay prudent with duration and limit the film to commercial parameters than get carried away and try and say everything with leisure. The finished film will be more conducive to commercial viewing and the audience will stay glued. No matter how dramatic or interesting the subject matter may be, no matter how well presented a narrative, an audience will lose patience after a while and start thinking about their dinner.

◆ ◆ ◆

7

WRITING A GREAT SCRIPT

What makes a good script? Yes, it is combining the various audiovisual and story elements together seamlessly. Yes, it is using story and script writing techniques in an effective way. Of course, it's having a good story to tell. The fact is, many scripts achieve this much. Most of them proceed to becoming good films too.

What makes a great script? That is a much harder question. Is it just the x-factor or can we pin-point certain things that have been noticed in award-winning films that go beyond the expected and set them apart from the ordinary? The answer is – we can. Anybody can make an award winning film. The key to this is just going that extra distance once the basics have been done and dusted.

Think!

It seems silly to ask a scriptwriter or filmmaker to really 'think' about his film. Of course he thinks about it – how could he not? However, does he really think enough? A great film is often a result of non-stop thinking about how it could be made great. The scriptwriter needs to go over everything related to his film over and over again in his mind and constantly challenge what he knows and how he thinks.

Then he should rethink the rethinking process! The idea behind what seems like excessive 'thinking' is that, sometime or the other, an inspired, creative and never-before-attempted idea will seep through to the surface and change the film dramatically. Is it really as simple as that? Sometimes it is.

Pulling on the Emotion string

One of the biggest misconceptions among documentary filmmakers is that, since documentaries deal in fact and are based in reality, there is a need to be more intellectual than emotional. This is based on the assumption that the kind of people who would be interested in non-fiction films would be the intellectuals within society. Emotion in documentary films is looked upon by such filmmakers with scorn, as if it were too 'pedestrian' to be taken seriously. The fact is, as a race, we humans are more emotional than intellectual. This includes everyone but an inconsequential minority. A film with a strong emotional flavour takes the audience along with it on its journey. To touch an audience member's mind may be to show him a great film, but to touch his heart is to ensure that he remembers it.

So go ahead – make them laugh, make them cry. Make them feel fear and pity, empathy and understanding. Make them celebrate gain and mourn loss along with the characters in the film. Make them nod vigorously along and shake their heads in disdain. Don't be afraid to include a variety of emotional elements in the film. A range of emotions will provide an unconscious feeling of 'completeness' within the audience.

This technique is often used in feature films to increase entertainment value. And, as many famous documentary filmmakers will tell you – there's nothing wrong with making an entertaining documentary.

Inspiring change once the lights have come on.

Never forget the message of your film. It is the reason behind the film project and the goal towards which an entire film unit has come to work together. Many people will, hopefully, spend time and money to watch your film after it is made. It is all for the message.

The idea of a documentary film is not only to showcase change, but to also inspire it. Documentary films are an effective tool in spurring people on to make social, political and issue-based changes in their own lives and communities. However, this desired response only takes place when the audience is inspired.

A great script makes sure not only that the audience hears and understands the message of the film loud and clear, but also creates in them the desire to be part of the solution and 'do' something as a follow up.

Therefore, the scriptwriter must tailor everything in the film in such a way that, when the lights come on in the screening room, every member of the audience has been inspired by the message of the film they've just seen and they go out into their own real lives with the conviction to change things for the better.

It's all in those telling details, those sudden surprises.

Imagine the Mona Lisa without that enigmatic smile. It is unthinkable. Out of millions of portraits painted over centuries, it is a simple smile, an expression that sets the Mona Lisa apart.

A documentary equivalent of the Mona Lisa, though yet to be made, would almost certainly contain that same element of detail that springs up to surprise and intrigue the audience. As a scriptwriter, it is important to research these details and find the ones that will add extra dimension and elements of surprise to the film. These details could be absolutely anything – from a gesture to an expression to an action to a detailed image to a sound choice.

They needn't be directly related to the subject and also needn't be covered excessively, but they can woven subtly into the fabric of the film. The choice of which details to use in the script is entirely up to the scriptwriter's imagination. It may help to think of dispensing these details as a form of 'playing' with the audience and staying a step ahead of them, anticipating every 'aha!' along the way.

No spoon feeding the audience. Challenge them!

It's easy to dispense information to the audience in a creative manner. It's also easy to tell them what to think as they go along in the story. The audience then becomes a passive observer to the events happening in the film. However, a great film makes sure that the audience is an active participant in the film process. The script should be structured in such a way that it questions the audience at every step, challenges their beliefs and encourages them to come to their own conclusions about events. Never say, "This is good" or "this is bad".

If you let the audience make that decision themselves, then they will feel more strongly about it. The basis for this argument is that every filmmaker or scriptwriter needs to have a healthy respect for his audience. If the film is targeted towards adults, then the scriptwriter must keep in mind that every person out there is a product of life experiences, has a mind of his own and has made important value-based decisions before. The scriptwriter needs to trust that an intelligent audience member will come to the right conclusion on his own.

Stand up for what you believe

The worst possible thing a scriptwriter can do is sit at his table just before writing a controversial sequence and think, "Maybe the audience won't like this. I should tone it down." The greatest films of all time weren't the 'toned down' ones.

In fact, some of the best documentaries ever made were Nazi propaganda films! A documentary film is a platform to express and challenge ideas and issues and the filmmaker should not be restricted by the desire to 'please' the audience. In fact, it is much better to have an audience up in arms, disagreeing strongly with the filmmaker's point of view, than to have a bored audience who leaves thinking that the film made no point at all. Stand up for your views, back them up with conclusive arguments and don't be afraid to believe in your film.

Experience your script in every way

Naturally, as the scriptwriter, you know the script you are writing well. However, have you experienced it? Every script is a film experience and a good scriptwriter is able to read the script he has written and experience it audio visually in his mind, going through exactly what the audience will go through and feeling as they would during every moment of the film. The idea behind this technique is to be able to fine tune the script in great detail and direct its energy along the way. This is a skill which comes with experience. However, a novice scriptwriter should learn to experience the following aspects of his script:

- He must experience the motivation behind every sequence in the film.
- He must know the type of energy, positive or negative, of every thought and idea expressed in all the individual shots.
- He must really know all the characters, central and secondary in the film.
- He must try and put himself in the audience's shoes and 'feel' their journey as the film progresses.

Be sensitive, be privileged

As a scriptwriter, you may or may not have met all the characters in your film or been to all the locations and experienced them. However, it is extremely important to remember that all the people and places you are writing about are real – they exist and have lives of their own. Lives, that they have allowed you and the film crew to enter and, in a sense, invade. They have given up not only their privacy, but put their reputation and honour in your hands. This is a privilege they have awarded you and you must always be aware of that responsibility. In return, you must treat them with respect and sensitivity and give them their due. Always, no matter how you feel about the subject personally, try and see things from their perspective. This attitude should apply to every character in the film, whether the film is eventually in agreement with their views or not.

Call it passion, call it inspiration

Needless to say, every person should be passionate about their work. However, often scriptwriters get bogged down by the extensive subject matter, structural elements and technical aspects that go into making a film and forget the spirit behind it. Filmmaking and film writing is all about passion – you must feel the spirit behind the subject matter and really want to put it out there for all to see. The closer you are to your script, the more imaginative and inspired you will be to try out new ideas and techniques and really make it special. Each script you write should be like a child you nurture while you work on it, each word you write should resonate with your passion. That is how masterpieces are made.

A word on simplicity

Coming back to the Mona Lisa; would she still be special if she were portrayed with the same expression but this time she was holding an infant on the back of a white horse galloping through fields of blazing fire in a charred landscape full of the souls of little children that looked like demons with their arms outstretched towards her baby?

Maybe, but, probably not. The point is, it doesn't have to be complicated to be good. In documentary, there is a tendency to make the narrative overly intellectual and complicated. This can, at best, make the film a little difficult to follow, and, at worst, alienate the audience. However, sometimes simplicity in word and thought can pull an audience far more effectively into the film experience.

A word on film shelf-life

A common problem with documentary films is their shelf life. A film within itself may be a suspension of space and time but after it's finished, it still has to exist in the real time of the real world. Documentaries often tend to deal with current events and issues and, in the real world, anything current today is outdated tomorrow. To ensure that a documentary has a reasonable shelf life of at least a few years, the filmmaker and scriptwriter need to ensure that there are no time-restrictive elements in the film. It always helps to address larger issues, which cannot be dated for a while. Date-specific events can be put into a larger context and the scriptwriter can, as far as possible, try to avoid putting the film into a very noticeable date in time.

◆ ◆ ◆

PART-II

FILM-SCREENPLAY

1

INTRODUCTION : FILM SCREENPLAY

A screenplay or script is a written work that is made especially for a film or television program. Screenplays can be original works or adaptations from existing pieces of writing. A play for television is known as a teleplay.

Screenwriting is the art and craft of writing scripts for film, television or video games.

Writing for film is potentially one of the most high-profile and best-paying careers available to a writer and, as such, is also perhaps the most sought after. It is increasingly difficult to make a living as a Hollywood screenwriter, as tens of thousands of people try every year. Yet it is still possible for a complete unknown to launch a career simply by writing a commercially-appealing screenplay and getting it into the hands of the right people.

Screenwriting in the entertainment industry

The act of screenwriting takes many forms across the entertainment industry. Often, multiple writers work on the same script at different stages of development with different tasks. Over the course of a successful career, a screenwriter might be hired to write in a wide variety of roles. Some of the most common forms of screenwriting jobs include:

- **Spec script writing**

  Spec scripts are feature film or television show scripts written on speculation, without the commission of a studio, production company, or network. The vast majority of scripts written each year are spec scripts, but only a small percentage make it to the screen. A spec script is usually a wholly original work, but can be an adaptation of an existing source.

In television writing, a spec script is a sample teleplay written to demonstrate the writer's knowledge of a show and ability to imitate its style and conventions. It is submitted to the show's producers in hopes of being hired to write future episodes of the show. Budding screenwriters attempting to break in to the business generally begin by writing one or more spec scripts.

Note that while writing "spec scripts" is part of any writer's career, the Writers Guild of America forbids members to write "on speculation" The distinction is that a "spec script" is written as a sample by the writer on his or her own; what is forbidden is writing a script for a specific producer without a contract.

- **Feature assignment writing**

Scripts written on assignment are screenplays created under contract with a studio, production company, or individual. Assignment scripts are generally adaptations of an existing idea or property owned by the hiring company, but can also be original works based on a concept created by the writer or producer.

Because assignments are created for hire, the writer typically has less creative freedom than on a spec script, and must meet specific criteria dictated by the producer.

- **Rewriting and script doctoring**

Most produced films are rewritten to some extent during the development process. Frequently, they are not rewritten by the original writer of the script.

Many established screenwriters, as well as new writers whose work shows promise but lacks marketability, make their living rewriting scripts.

When a script's central premise or characters are good

but the script is otherwise unusable, a different writer or team of writers is contracted to do an entirely new draft, often referred to as a "page one rewrite." When only small problems remain, such as bad dialogue or poor humor, a writer is hired to do a "polish" or "punch-up".

Depending on the size of the new writer's contributions, screen credit may or may not be given.

For instance, in the American film industry, credit to rewriters is given only if 50% or more of the script is substantially changed. These standards can make it difficult to establish the identity and number of screenwriters who contributed to a film's creation.

When an established, successful writer is called in to rewrite portions of a script late in the development process, they are commonly referred to as script doctors. Prominent script doctors include William Goldman, Robert Towne, Mort Nathan, and Quentin Tarantino.

- **Television writing**

A freelance television writer uses spec scripts or their previous credits and reputation to get contracted by an existing tv show to write one or more episodes. After the episode is written, the teleplay is submitted to the network and rewriting or polishing may be required.

Subsequent drafts of the script may be done by the freelancer or by the show's staff.

A staff writer for a television show generally works in-house writing and rewriting episodes for the show. Staff writers - often given other titles, such as story editor, or producer - work both as a group and individually on episode scripts to maintain the show's tone, style, characters, and plots. Television show creators, also known as show runners, write the pilot episode and bible of a new television series.

They are responsible for creating and managing all aspects of a show's characters, style, and plots. Frequently, a creator remains responsible for the show's day-to-day creative decisions throughout the series run.

- **Writing for soap operas**

  The process of writing for soap operas is different than that used by prime time shows, due in part to the need to produce new episodes five days a week, fifty-two weeks a year. In one example cited by Jane Espenson, screenwriting is a "sort of three-tiered system":

  a few top writers craft the overall story arcs. Mid-level writers work with them to turn those arcs into things that look a lot like traditional episode outlines, and an array of writers below that (who do not even have to be local to Los Angeles), take those outlines and quickly generate the dialogue while adhering slavishly to the outlines.

  Espenson notes that a recent trend has been to eliminate the role of the mid-level writer, relying on the senior writers to do rough outlines and giving the other writers a bit more freedom. Regardless, when the finished scripts are sent to the top writers, the latter do a final round of rewrites.

  Espenson also notes that a show that airs daily with characters that have decades of history behind their voices necessitates a writing staff without the distinctive voice that can sometimes be present of prime-time series.

- **Writing for game shows**

  Game shows feature live contestants, but still use a team of writers as part of a specific format. This may involve the slate of questions, and even specific phrasing or dialogue on the part of the host. Writers may not script the dialogue used by the contestants, but they work with the producers to create the actions, scenarios, and sequence of events that support the game show's concept.

- **Video game writing**

  With the continued development and increased complexity of video games, many opportunities are available to screenwriters in the field of video game design. Video game writers work closely with the other game designers to create characters, scenarios, and dialogue.

Theories on writing a screenplay

Fundamentally, the screenplay is a unique literary form. It is like a musical score, in that it is intended to be interpreted on the basis of other artists' performance, rather than serving as a "finished product" for the enjoyment of its audience. For this reason, a screenplay is written using technical jargon and tight, spare prose when describing stage directions. Unlike a novel or short story, a screenplay focuses on describing the literal, visual aspects of the story, rather than on the internal thoughts of its characters. In screenwriting, the aim is to evoke those thoughts and emotions through subtext, action, and symbolism.

There are several main screenwriting theories which help writers approach the screenplay by systematizing the structure, goals and techniques of writing a script. The most common kinds of theories are structural. Screenwriter William Goldman is widely quoted as saying "Screenplays are structure".

Three act structure

Most screenplays have a three act structure, following an organization that dates back to Aristotle's Poetics and developed with respect to feature films by Syd Field, author of Screenplay and The Screen Writer's Workbook. The three acts are setup (of the location and characters), confrontation (with an obstacle), and resolution (culminating in a climax and a dénouement). In a two-hour film, the first and third acts typically last 30 minutes, with the middle act lasting an hour.

In Writing Drama, French writer and director Yves Lavandier shows a slightly different approach.. As most theorists, he maintains that every human action, whether fictitious or real, contains three logical parts: before the action, during the action, and after the action. But since the climax is part of the action, Yves Lavandier considers the second act must include the climax. Which makes for a much shorter third act than what is found in most screenwriting theories.

Besides the three act structure, one could also use four or even five acts in a screenplay, though these would be used to suit longer stories than the classic 120 page format.

The Hero's Journey

The Hero's Journey, also referred to as the Monomyth, is an idea formulated by noted mythologist Joseph Campbell. The central concept of the Monomyth is that a pattern can be seen in stories and myths across history. Campbell defined and explained that pattern in his book The Hero with a Thousand Faces(1949).

Campbell's insight was that important myths from around the world which have survived for thousands of years, all share a fundamental structure. This fundamental structure contains a number of stages, which includes

- A call to adventure, which the hero has to accept or decline
- A road of trials, regarding which the hero succeeds or fails
- Achieving the goal or "boon," which often results in important self-knowledge
- A return to the ordinary world, again as to which the hero can succeed or fail
- Application of the boon, in which what the hero has gained can be used to improve the world

Later, screenwriter Christopher Vogler refined and expanded the Hero's Journey for the screenplay form in his book, The Writer's Journey: Mythic Structure for Writers(1993).

Syd Field's Paradigm

Screenwriting guru Syd Field wrote the seminal book Screenplay, and posited a new theory, which he called the Paradigm. Field noticed that in a 120-page screenplay, Act Two was notoriously boring, and was also twice the length of Acts One and Three. He also noticed that an important dramatic event usually occurred at the middle of the picture, which implied to him that the middle act was actually two acts in one. So the Three Act Structure is notated 1, 2a, 2b, 3, resulting in Aristotle's Three Acts divided into four pieces.

Field also introduced the idea of Plot Points into screenwriting theory. Plot Points are important structural functions that happen in approximately the same place in most successful movies, like the verses and choruses in a popular song. In subsequent books, Field has added to his original list, and students of his like Viki King and Linda Seger have added to the list of Plot Points. Here is a current list of the major Plot Points that are congruent with Field's Paradigm:

- ***Opening Image:*** The first image in the screenplay should summarize the entire film, especially its tone. Often, writers go back and redo this as the last thing before submitting the script.

- ***Inciting Incident:*** Also called the catalyst, this is the point in the story when the Protagonist encounters the problem that will change their life. This is when the detective is assigned the case, where Boy meets Girl, and where the Comic Hero gets fired from his cushy job, forcing him into comic circumstances.

- ***Plot Point 1:*** The last scene in Act One, Turning Point One is a surprising development that radically changes the Protagonist's life, and forces him to confront the Opponent. In Star Wars, this is when Luke's family is killed by the Empire. He has no home to go back to, so he joins the Rebels in opposing Darth Vader.

- ***Pinch 1:*** A reminder scene at about 3/8 the way through the script (halfway through Act 2a) that brings up the central conflict of the drama, reminding us of the overall conflict. For example, in Star Wars, Pinch 1 is the Stormtroopers attacking the Millennium Falcon in Mos Eisley, reminding us the Empire is after the stolen plans to the Death Star R2-D2 is carrying and Luke and Ben Kenobi are trying to get to the Rebel Alliance (the main conflict).

• ***Midpoint:*** An important scene in the middle of the script, often a reversal of fortune or revelation that changes the direction of the story. Field suggests that driving the story towards the Midpoint keeps the second act from sagging.

• ***Pinch 2:*** Another reminder scene about 5/8 through the script (halfway through Act 2b) that is somehow linked to Pinch 1 in reminding the audience about the central conflict. In Star Wars, Pinch 2 is the Stormtroopers attacking them as they rescue the Princess in the Death Star. Both scenes remind us of the Empire's opposition, and using the Stormtrooper attack motif unifies both Pinches.

• ***Plot Point 2:*** A dramatic reversal that ends Act 2 and begins Act 3, which is about confrontation and resolution. Sometimes Turning Point Two is the moment when the Hero has had enough and is finally going to face the Opponent. Sometimes, like in Toy Story, it's the low-point for the Hero, and he must bounce back to overcome the odds in Act 3.

• ***Showdown:*** About midway through Act 3, the Protagonist will confront the Main Problem of the story and either overcome it, or come to a tragic end.

• ***Resolution:*** The issues of the story are resolved.

• ***Tag:*** An epilogue, tying up the loose ends of the story, giving the audience closure. This is also known as denouement. In general, films in recent decades have had longer denouements than films made in the 1970s or earlier.

The sequence approach

The sequence approach to screenwriting, sometimes known as "eight-sequence structure", is a system developed by Frank Daniel, while he was the head of the Graduate Screenwriting Program at USC. It is based in part on the fact that, in the early days of cinema, technical matters forced screenwriters to divide their stories into sequences, each the length of a reel (about ten minutes).

The sequence approach mimics that early style. The story is broken up into eight 10-15 minute sequences. The sequences serve as "mini-movies", each with their own compressed three-act structure. The first two sequences combine to form the film's first act. The next four create the film's second act. The final two sequences complete the resolution and dénouement of the story. Each sequence's resolution creates the situation which sets up the next sequence.

Screenwriting formats

Screenplays and teleplays have set of standardizations in place, beginning with proper formatting. These rules are in part to serve the practical purpose of making scripts uniformly readable "blueprints" of movies, and also to serve as a way of distinguishing a professional from an amateur. It is very important that the correct format is used, as the script is likely to be disregarded very quickly. There are practical reasons for this. An incorrectly formatted script can be very difficult for actors to read from, when testing the script out. If you are unsure exactly what is required, then at least be consistent, and keep things as simple as possible.

Feature film

Motion picture screenplays intended for submission to mainstream studios, whether in the US or elsewhere in the world, are expected to conform to a standard typographical style known widely as studio format which stipulates how elements of the screenplay such as scene headings, action, transitions, dialog, character names, shots and parenthetical matter should be presented on the page, as well as the font size and line spacing.

One reason for this is that, when rendered in studio format, most screenplays will transfer onto the screen at the rate of approximately one page per minute. This rule of thumb is widely contested — a page of dialog usually occupies less screen time than a page of action, for example, and it depends enormously on the literary style of the writer — and yet it continues to hold sway in modern Hollywood.

There is no single standard for studio format. Some studios have definitions of the required format written into the rubric of their writer's contract. The Nicholl Fellowship, a screenwriting competition run under the auspices of the Academy of Motion Picture Arts and Sciences, has a useful and accurate guide to screenplay format. Screenplays are traditionally 90-120 pages long. Comedies and children's films tend to weigh in at the lower end.Screenplays are almost always written using a monospaced font, often a variant of Courier or Courier New, both mostly used as 12 pt font.

Television

For Indian TV shows, the format rules for hour-long dramas, like Bidai, Kahani Ghar-Ghar ki and single-camera sitcoms, like Bandini, are essentially the same as for motion pictures. The main difference is that TV scripts have act breaks. Multi-camera sitcoms, like I Love Lucy and "Seinfeld", use a different, specialized format that derives from radio and the stage play. In this format, dialogue is double-spaced, action lines are capitalized, and scene headings are capitalized and underlined.

Drama series and sitcoms are no longer the only formats that require the skills of a writer. With reality-based programming crossing genres to create various hybrid programs, many of the so-called "reality" programs are in a large part scripted in format. That is, the overall skeleton of the show and its episodes are written to dictate the content and direction of the program. The Writers Guild has identified this as a legitimate writer's medium, so much so that they have lobbied to impose jurisdiction over writers and producers who "format" reality-based productions. Creating reality show formats involves storytelling structure similar to screenwriting, but much more condensed and boiled down to specific plot points or actions related to the overall concept and story.

Documentaries

The script format for documentaries and audio-visual presentations which consist largely of voice-over matched to still or moving pictures is different again and uses a two-column format which can be particularly difficult to achieve in standard word processors, at least when it comes to editing. Many script-editing software programs include templates for documentary formats.

Physical format

Indian screenplays are printed single-sided on three-hole-punched A-4 sized paper, and held together with two brass brads in the top and bottom hole. The middle hole is left empty. In the UK, double-hole-punched A4 paper is often used, although some UK writers use the US letter paper format, especially when their scripts are to be read by American producers, since otherwise the pages may be cropped when printed on US paper. Despite the use of double-punched paper, it is common to see scripts in the UK held together by a single brad punched in the top left hand corner. This makes it easy to flip from page to page during script meetings and may have something to do with the taller page of A4.

Screenplays are usually bound with a light card stock cover and back page, often showing the logo of the production company or agency submitting the script.

Increasingly, reading copies of screenplays (that is, those distributed by producers and agencies in the hope of attracting finance or talent) are distributed printed on both sides of the paper (often professionally bound) to cut down on paper waste out of environmental concerns. Occasionally they are reduced to half-size to make a small book which is convenient to read or put in a pocket; this is generally for use by the director or other production crew during shooting.

Although most writing contracts continue to stipulate physical delivery of three or more copies of a finished script, it is common for scripts to be delivered electronically via email. Although most production companies can handle scripts in most formats, it is better practice to supply scripts as a PDF file where possible. This is because it gives the writer final control over the layout of the script, which may otherwise vary depending on what fonts and/or paper size the recipient uses to print the script out. The formatting software programs listed at the bottom of this article produce industry formatted standard screenplays in PDF.

Imagery

Imagery can be used in many metaphoric ways. In The Talented Mr. Ripley, the title character talked of wanting to close the door on himself sometime, and then, in the end, he did. Rain is commonly used to express a character feeling depressed, while sunny days promote a feeling of happiness and calm. Imagery can be used to sway the emotions of the audience and to clue them in to what is happening. Imagery is well defined in City of God. The opening image sequence sets the tone for the entire film. The film opens with the shimmer of a knife's blade on a sharpening stone. A drink is being prepared, The knife's blade shows again, juxtaposed is a shot of a chicken letting loose of its harness on its feet. All symbolising 'The One that got away'. The film is about life in the favelas in Rio - sprinkled with violence and games and ambition.

Dialogue

Dialogue is very important to the film industry, because there are no written words to explain the characters or plot; it all has to be explained through dialogue and imagery.

Plot

While the story is what will be told (narrative); the plot is how the story will be told (narration). This vocabulary is not indisputable, though. Sometimes in literature story and plot are used exactly the other way round.

◆ ◆ ◆

2

SHOOTING SCRIPT

A shooting script is the version of a screenplay used during the production of a motion picture. Shooting scripts are distinct from spec scripts in that they make use of scene numbers (along with certain other formatting conventions described below), and they follow a well defined set of procedures specifying how script revisions should be implemented and circulated.

Overview

When a screenplay is approved for production, the scenes are assigned numbers which are included in the script alongside the scene headers. The numbers provide a convenient way for the various production departments to reference individual scenes.

After a shooting script has been widely circulated, page numbers are locked, and any revisions are distributed on revision pages. Thus the production office might issue a revision containing new pages 3, 9, 17 and 45. This avoids having to print and distribute an entirely new draft for every set of revisions, which would entail crew members having to transfer all their handwritten notes to a new script. If scenes on page 45 become longer, they will be continued on new pages 45A, 45B and so on; if the scenes on page 45 are all eliminated, a new page 45 will be issued with the word "OMIT" as the absence of a page 45 might look like an error.

Revision pages are distributed on colored paper, a different color for each set of revisions, with each changed line marked by an asterisk in the right margin of the page. The progression of colors varies from one production to the next, but a typical sequence would be: white, blue, pink, yellow, green, gold, salmon, cherry, white (this time known as "double white"), and back to blue ("double blue").

When the Assistant Director believes that there are more changed pages than are worth swapping out, the Script Coordinator may issue an entirely fresh script in the appropriate revision color. In some cases, usually before the start of principal photography, an entirely new "white draft" will be distributed in lieu of colored revision pages. The pages in a white draft are renumbered from scratch, while the original scene numbers are maintained.

Preserving scene and page numbers

When revisions are made to a shooting script, they must be accomplished in a way that doesn't disturb the pre-existing scene numbers. For example, if a new scene is to be inserted between scenes 10 and 11, the new scene will be numbered 10A. Every scene thus retains its own unique number throughout the course of the production. When a scene is omitted, its number is preserved in the script along with the phrase (OMITTED). This effectively retires the number so that it can't be reused by a new scene inserted later at the same location.

Page numbers in a shooting script are handled in a similar way. When revision pages are distributed, the page numbers must flow sequentially into the pre-existing page numbers. For example, if page 10 is revised such that it now occupies a page and a half, the revisions will be distributed on two pages numbered 10 and 10A. These two pages will replace page 10 in the outstanding drafts. Conversely, if pages 15 and 16 are shortened such that they now occupy a single page, the revisions will be distributed on a single page numbered 15-16.

Sequence

In film, a sequence is a series of scenes which form a distinct narrative unit, usually connected either by unity of location or unity of time. For example a heist film might include an extended recruitment sequence in which the leader of the gang collects together the conspirators, a robbery sequence, an escape sequence, and so on. Each of these sequences might further contain sub-sequences; for example the robbery sequence might consist of an entry sequence, a safe-cracking sequence, and so on.

The sequence is one of a hierarchy of structural units used to describe the structure of films in varying degrees of granularity. Analysed this way, a film is composed of one or more acts; acts include one or more sequences; sequences comprise one or more scenes; and scenes may be thought of as being built out of shots (if one is thinking visually) or beats (if one is thinking in narrative terms).

The sequence paradigm of screenwriting was developed by Frank Daniel.

Post-credits scene

A post-credits scene (also called a stinger, tag, or movie coda) is a short clip that appears after some or all of the closing credits of a film have run. It is usually either included for humor (where it may be called a "stinger gag") or to set up a possible sequel, as well as to inspire the audience to stay through the credits during the theatrical release.

The use of stingers may be traced back to the 1963 James Bond film, From Russia with Love, which was the first in the series to show the ubiquitous "James Bond will return in..." at the end of the credits. The 1978 film Superman featured a tagline promoting the film's sequel, due out the following year. However, these were simply text at the end of the credits, and did not include clips or teasers from the upcoming films (although the original shooting script for Superman contained a stinger that featured General Zod, Ursa, and Non being freed from the Phantom Zone following the credits).

One of the earliest appearances of a true stinger in a main-stream film was in The Muppet Movie in 1979, and use of such scenes gained popularity throughout the 1980s at the end of comedy films. The Muppet Movie also began a trend of using such stingers to break the fourth wall, even when much of the rest of the film had kept it intact. The scenes were often used as a form of metafiction, with characters showing an awareness that they were at the end of a film, and often telling the audience directly to leave the theatre. Films using this technique include Ferris Bueller's Day Off (in which the title character frequently broke the fourth wall during the movie) and The Producers (in which it was not so common). The stinger of the latter movie also includes the film's only cameo appearance of producer Mel Brooks. Stingers also appeared on the long-running TV show Mystery Science Theater 3000, introduced in episode 205 ("Rocket Attack USA"), continuing until the end of the series. The stingers, with a few exceptions, highlighted moments from the films that were either particularly nonsensical or had simply caught the Brains' attention.

The 1903 film The Great Train Robbery ends with leader of the outlaw band taking aim and firing point blank at the audience (after having been killed in the previous scene). After the credits of 1985's "Young Sherlock Holmes", the villainous schoolmaster Rathe is revealed to have survived his drowning and taken the name Professor James Moriarty.

Modern examples

Stingers lacking the metafictional aspects also gained prominence in the 1980s, although they were still primarily used for comedy films. Post-credits scenes became useful places for humorous scenes that would not fit in the main body of the film. Most were short clips that served to tie together loose ends—minor characters whose fates were not elaborated on earlier in the movie, or plotlines that were not fully wrapped up. At the end of the Disney animated made-for-video film Aladdin: The Return of Jafar, Abis Mal asks for his third wish; in its sequel, towards the end of the song "Welcome to the Forty Thieves", which plays over the credits, the Genie is seen squished between the black background and the credits with a bit of dialogue at the very end. During its wide release, Napoleon Dynamite features a stinger that reveals that Kip and LaFawnduh get married. The film version of Harry Potter and the Chamber of Secrets features a stinger showing a poster at a book store for a new book by Gilderoy Lockhart (who accidentally wiped his memory earlier in the movie) entitled "Who Am I?" Also, in the Pirates of the Caribbean films, there is a scene that usually connects to another story. The first movie ended with Jack (the monkey) becoming cursed after removing a medallion from the Aztec chest. The second movie ended with the dog from the jail being the new god of the native tribe. The third movie ended with Elizabeth and her son witnessing Will's return from the sea.

Even when post-credit scenes started to be used by films with little comedy development, the same format of giving closure to incomplete storylines or inconsequential characters remained in use. Using humor in such scenes is also still common for more serious films, as in the film Daredevil, in which Bullseye is shown after his defeat by Daredevil in a full body cast. Another example happens in Hellboy when Tom Manning is shown still wandering around the catacombs when he was last seen previously in the film when the other major players have left. Other films eschew the comedy in favor of a twist or revelation that would be out of place elsewhere in the movie, as in X-Men: The Last Stand's post-credits scene, which suggests that Professor X may have transferred his mind to the body of a comatose patient (which was revealed in the DVD commentary to be the identical twin of Charles Xavier, whose mind had been crippled and destroyed due to Charles's growing powers in their mother's womb). In Iron Man, Samuel L. Jackson makes a cameo appearance as Nick Fury, who wants to talk to Tony Stark about the "Avenger Initiative" (Jackson will reprise the role in other Marvel films, including The Avengers, Iron Man 2, Thor, and The First Avenger: Captain America).

At the end of the credits in the 2006 film Cars, Mini and Van were shown on screen for a few seconds, saying they were lost.

Scene continueds

When a numbered scene is split across pages, (CONTINUED) appears at the bottom of the prior page, and CONTINUED: appears at the top of the subsequent page. This continued indicator appears along with the number of the scene being continued and a bracketed count of how often the scene has been continued thus far, e.g. 107 CONTINUED: (2). The number is usually omitted when it's equal to one.

Dialogue continueds

When dialogue is split across pages, (MORE) appears below the portion of dialogue on the first page, similar to a parenthetical but indented the same as the character's name. On the subsequent page, the remaining dialogue is headed by the character's name, which is extended by an abbreviated continued indicator, e.g. JOHN (CONT'D).

When a character speaks more than once consecutively, with only action separating the speeches, (continuing) parentheticals can be used in the subsequent speeches. (continuing) parentheticals are positioned the same as standard ones: below the character's name and indented from the dialogue. Some writers indicate consecutive dialogue by including (CONT'D) beside the character's name (the same as for dialogue split across pages). Many writers choose not to indicate consecutive dialogue at all.

Dialogue continueds apply to both spec and production scripts. They are mentioned here because of the confusion that arises over the many uses of continued.

The revision slug

A slug (header) appears at the top of every revision page, aligned vertically with the page number. The revision slug typically includes the date the revisions were circulated, the color of the pages in parentheses, and usually, the name of the production or some other descriptive information. Every set of revisions is distributed along with a title page that includes a list of the revision slugs for every set of revisions distributed thus far.

Revision marks

Script revisions are marked with asterisks in the right hand margins of the revision pages. When many revision marks are present on a single page, or within a single paragraph or scene, the marks may be consolidated into a single mark. For example, if all the lines in a given passage of dialogue are marked, the marks can be consolidated into a single mark appearing alongside the name of the speaker above the dialogue. In the case of scenes, this single "consolidation mark" appears alongside the scene header. For pages, the consolidation mark appears beside the page number.

Screenplay slug line

A slug line is unique to the screenplay and states numerous things about a scene. Often called a Master Scene Heading, it occurs at the start of every scene, and is usually made up of three parts.

Part one

Part one states if the scene is set inside (interior) or outside (exterior). The abbreviations INT. and EXT. are used. A period always follows each abbreviation.

Sometimes the scene may move from interior to exterior several times within a scene. In the interest of brevity, the writer may choose to use INT./EXT. or EXT./INT.

Part two

Part two states the location of the scene, such as GOVINDA`S APARTMENT, PRIDE ROCK or BATHROOM. After the location, a space hyphen space occurs. If the location needs to be more specific, then a space hyphen space can occur, followed by the more specific place. For example: SANJANA'S APARTMENT - KITCHEN. A space hyphen space is still needed after this to separate it from part three.

Part three

Part three refers to the time of the scene. Day or Night are normally used, but Dusk, Dawn, Late Night, Early Morning and others can be used if necessary. For example, if a particular scene requires a sunrise, Dawn can be used.

If a character starts inside, and then walks outside during a scene, a new slug line will be needed, but in this slug line, 'Continuous' will be written instead.

'Later' can be used to indicate the passage of time.

Examples

Here are some examples of slug lines, and shows how all the parts fit together.

INT. GOVINDA'S APARTMENT - DAY

EXT. PARK - NIGHT

INT. SANJANA'S APARTMENT - KITCHEN - NIGHT

EXT. BEACH - DAWN

INT./EXT. TOOL SHED - DAY

Variations

Variations do occur to this. One slug line used in the pilot for Arrested Development reads:

HEADSHOT

of Tobias in newspaper.

The slug line in this instance is merely HEADSHOT, which leads into the action line (which is the 'of Tobias in newspaper' part) These variations are used only when they are needed, such as when photos are shown, and sometimes when computer or television screens are shown.

Another variation occurs when a scene takes place in an unusual location. For example, 'Space' can be used in place of the time of day if the scene doesn't take place on a planet:

EXT. FEDERATION BATTLESHIP - AREBIAN BAY - SPACE

Secondary Headings

These offshoots of slug lines allow the writer to shift the action without the waste of space of a full heading. The master scene heading can give the general location:

INT. RAJEEV'S HOUSE - DAY

Then a secondary heading can be used to indicate that the action is moving to a new location within the house, such as

JITENDRA'S BEDROOM

or

KITCHEN

Scene numbering

Each slug line begins a new scene. In a shooting script, the slug lines are numbered consecutively. These scene numbers serve as mile-post markers in a script. This allows any part of the script to be referred to by scene number. Do not confuse these scenes with shooting sequences.

Accepted Practices

Formatting variations are generally accepted as long as the intent is clear, but a few rules do exist:

1. Any change of time or location requires a new slug line.

2. All slug lines are on their own lines, flush with the left margin, and typed in all capital letters.

3. Master scene heading can not be the last item on a page. It must be followed by at least one line of description or dialogue.

4. The writer may double or triple space before the slug line, but should always double space afterward.

◆ ◆ ◆

3

SCRIPTMENT

A scriptment is a written work by a movie or television screenwriter that combines elements of a script and treatment, especially the dialogue elements, which are formatted the same as in a screenplay. It is a more elaborate document than a standard draft treatment. A lengthy scriptment may resemble a script sufficiently to be used as the basis for qualifying the writer to receive or share a screenplay credit, as opposed to just a story credit. Some films have been shot using only a scriptment.

The term scriptment was originally coined by filmmaker James Cameron, possibly during his early involvement in the development of the Spider-Man film series. In that effort, after the success of his 1984 film The Terminator, Cameron wrote a 47-page scriptment for the first proposed Spider-man movie, which was used by screenwriter David Koepp to write the first draft, incorporating it nearly word for word.

Cameron's scriptment for Titanic was 131 pages. The term became more widely known, when Cameron's 1995 scriptment for the film Avatar was leaked on the internet during pre-production, although other directors, such as John Hughes and Zak Penn, had written "scriptments" before. The scriptment for Avatar was 80 pages and reportedly Cameron wrote it in just two weeks.

Elements

A scriptment borrows characteristics from both a regular screenplay and a film treatment and is comparable to a step outline: the main text body is similar to an elaborate draft treatment, while usually only major sequences receive scene location headings (slug lines), which is different from the extensive slug line formatting in standard screenplays, where every new scene or shot begins with an INT./EXT. DAY/NIGHT slug line set above the description or dialogue. However, just as a treatment can be short or long, a scriptment can exist in various degrees of completion depending on how much time the writer has devoted to it and a more fully developed one could have all slug lines in place, a great deal of dialogue, and only require the producer's (or a writing partner's) okay on the direction the finished script should take before proceeding further.

In a scriptment, scenes and shots may be separated as paragraphs or sentences and, if it is the writer's style, can also include an occasional explanatory note, such as might be important in an adaptation or a sequel. As with standard treatments, much of the dialogue is summarized in action. The longer the scriptment, however, the more likely it contains dialog scenes that are fully developed. Single words or brief phrases of dialogue can be included within the description and lengthier exchanges are formatted exactly as a regular screenplay, which is the main reason for the "script" part of the term.

The longer the scriptment, the more likely it is written shot to shot as opposed to scene by scene; thus, a long, detailed scriptment does not necessarily equate to a longer movie, as a typical 90-120 page screenplay written with master scenes contains many more individual shots than are immediately apparent.

A scriptment can begin with FADE IN: top left and conclude with a centered THE END. It can have a title page like a script and lengthier treatment. It is written single spaced with an empty space between paragraphs and other elements and the pages are numbered in the upper right corner, just as in a screenplay.

Work-in-progress manuscript

Directors and screenwriters write scriptments as an intermediate stage in development from the draft treatment to the first draft of the screenplay. Like a draft treatment, a scriptment can be anywhere from 20 to 80 or more pages. While regular presentation treatments or outlines only summarize the plot, typically in not more than 30 pages.

- For the Batman feature film The Dark Knight, writer David S. Goyer and the film's director Christopher Nolan wrote a scriptment that was then used by Nolan and his brother Jonathan Nolan to expand further into a finished screenplay. "I wrote what you'd call a 'scriptment' with Chris over an accelerated month long period, and then we handed it off to his brother [Jonathan], who did the first pass," explains Goyer.
- The sci-fi movie Transformers: Revenge of the Fallen reportedly used a scriptment during the screenplay writing process by Roberto Orci, Alex Kurtzman, Ehren Kruger and director Michael Bay.
- Filmmaker Wayne Spitzer used a scriptment while writing the adaptation of author Algernon Blackwood's 1907 supernatural short story "The Willows".
- Comic book writer Warren Ellis has written that he sometimes works in the scriptment style.

Recently, writers outside of the film industry have begun to use scriptments as rough drafts for their novels, sketching early scenes and such, and later completely fleshing them out and dividing them into chapters. It can cut planning time in half, as it gives them a chance to not only flesh but test outlines, in as little as two weeks.

Presentation manuscript

A scriptment can also be a presentation document; that is, one that is sold or handed in as the finished work.

- Writer-director-producer James Cameron delivered a 47-page scriptment that he was contracted to write during the development phase of the first Spider-Man (2002) theatrical movie, which he was also going to direct. When Cameron left the project, screenwriter David Koepp expanded it into a first draft script, which was later worked on by other uncredited writers.

• In 2005, Sony Pictures paid screenwriter Ken Nolan US $3 million for his 75-page scriptment that was an adaptation of the then-unpublished Whitley Strieber novel The Grays. Nolan had only one produced writing credit at the time, the screenplay for the military film Black Hawk Down, a project for which he had submitted three different scriptments to producer Jerry Bruckheimer and executive producers Mike Stenson, and Chad Oman for approval during the writing process.

• The movie Cloverfield written by Drew Goddard, directed by Matt Reeves, and produced by J. J. Abrams, was greenlighted for production by Paramount Pictures President of Production Brad Weston and Brad Grey, Chairman, based on a 65-page scriptment. The film was also shot using the scriptment.

• Director-producer-writer John Hughes wrote a 70-page scriptment for the Owen Wilson-starring comedy Drillbit Taylor that was used years later by screenwriters Kristofor Brown and Seth Rogen as the basis for a revised finished screenplay.

• The 2009 comedy film I Love You, Beth Cooper, written by Larry Doyle, originated as an 85-page scriptment that was shopped around Hollywood and then subsequently turned into a book manuscript.

• The improv comedy movie The Grand, written by Zak Penn and Matt Bierman, was filmed using a scriptment.

• Also using a scriptment for filming was the 2008 comedy Reno 911!: Miami, written by Robert Ben Garant, Thomas Lennon, and Kerri Kenney-Silver.

• Filmmakers Kriv Stenders and Richard Green used the scripment format to make their 2007 film Boxing Day.

- It was reported on the movie news website Ain't It Cool News on December 1, 2008 that a scriptment was involved in developing a possible new Speed sequel or remake: "There's a scriptment floating around that reintroduces Jack Traven. So the studios are hoping to get Keanu back on board."

Film treatment

A film treatment (or treatment for short) is a piece of prose, typically the step between scene cards (index cards) and the first draft of a screenplay for a motion picture, television program, or radio play. It is generally longer and more detailed than an outline (or one-page synopsis) and shorter and less detailed than a step outline, but it may include details of directorial style that an outline omits. They read like a short story, except told in the present tense and describing events as they happen. There are two types: the original draft treatment, created during the writing process, and the presentation treatment, created as presentation material.

Original draft treatment

Generally long and detailed. It's compiled of full-scene outlines put together. These are usually more than about 30 standard letter/A4 pages (Courier New 12 point), less than about 80 pages, and an average of about 40 pages. For example, The Terminator original treatment is 44 pages. More elaborate forms of the draft treatment are the step outline and the scriptment.

Presentation treatment

Generally the scene card descriptions are written out in order. These only have the essential and important story events that make up the scenes. It's the full story in its simplest form. Usually starting with the Concept, then the Theme, then Character, and also the detailed synopsis of about 4 - 8 pages of master scenes. This is either to show how the production notes have been incorporated into the screenplay for the director and production executives to look over, or to leave behind as a presentation note after a sales pitch. This would be the treatment to send if a script submission requires one. These are usually more than about 3 pages, less than about 30 pages, and an average of 7-12 pages.

Treatments are widely used within the motion picture industry as selling documents, whereas outlines are generally produced as part of the development process.

Screenwriters may use a treatment to initially pitch a screenplay, but may also use a treatment to sell a concept they are pitching without a completed screenplay. In 2009, Nicholas Jarecki started a website called beatsheetcentral.com to collect treatments (beat sheets) for the plots of existing movies and television episodes.

Script breakdown

A script breakdown is an intermediate step in the production of a play, film, comic book, or any other work that is originally planned using a script. In film and television, a script breakdown is: a) an analysis of a screenplay in which all of the production elements are reduced to lists in order to schedule and budget the production; b) a director's creative analysis of the dramatic action, reciprocal struggle, theme, and design elements of a screenplay.

Comics

In comic books, it is the process of determining how each action, character, and piece of dialogue described in the script will be placed visually on a page. In the studio system that dominated mass-market comic-book production from the 1940s through the 1970s, breakdowns were done by the penciller or by a separate breakdown artist, rarely by the scriptwriter; in some cases, breakdowns were done from a rough story outline before the dialogue was written (the "Marvel method"). Later comics writers such as Alan Moore and Neil Gaiman, influenced by cinematic technique, began to include more layout details within their scripts. Cartoonists who both write and draw their own work sometimes begin with a script and do their own breakdowns, and sometimes work through drawings without a separate script.

◆ ◆ ◆

4

STORYBOARD

Storyboards are graphic organizers such as a series of illustrations or images displayed in sequence for the purpose of pre-visualizing a motion picture, animation, motion graphic or interactive media sequence, including website interactivity.

The storyboarding process, in the form it is known today, was developed at the Walt Disney Studio during the early 1930s, after several years of similar processes being in use at Walt Disney and other animation studios.

The storyboarding process can be very tedious and intricate. The form widely known today was developed at the Walt Disney studio during the early 1930s. In the biography of her father, The Story of Walt Disney (Henry Holt, 1956), Diane Disney Miller explains that the first complete storyboards were created for the 1933 Disney short Three Little Pigs. According to John Canemaker, in Paper Dreams: The Art and Artists of Disney Storyboards (1999, Hyperion Press), the first storyboards at Disney evolved from comic-book like "story sketches" created in the 1920s to illustrate concepts for animated cartoon short subjects such as Plane Crazy and Steamboat Willie.

According to Christopher Finch in The Art of Walt Disney (Abrams, 1974), Disney credited animator Webb Smith with creating the idea of drawing scenes on separate sheets of paper and pinning them up on a bulletin board to tell a story in sequence, thus creating the first storyboard.

One of the first live action films to be completely storyboarded was Gone with the Wind. William Cameron Menzies, the film's production designer, was hired by David Selznick to design every shot of the film. Many large budget silent films were also storyboarded but most of this material has been lost during the reduction of the studio archives during the 1970s.

Storyboarding became popular in live-action film production during the early 1940s, and grew into a standard medium for previsualization of films: "We can see the last half century .... as the period in which production design was largely characterized by adoption of the storyboard", wrote curator Annette Michelson in a 1993 catalog for the Pace Gallery exhibit Drawing into Film: Director's Drawings, which featured storyboards of popular films. Storyboards are now an essential part of the creation progress.

Storyboarding's most recent use is outlining websites and other interactive media projects during the design phase.

Usage

- ***Film***

  A film storyboard is essentially a large comic of the film or some section of the film produced beforehand to help film directors, cinematographers and television commercial advertising clients visualize the scenes and find potential problems before they occur. Often storyboards include arrows or instructions that indicate movement.

  In creating a motion picture with any degree of fidelity to a script, a storyboard provides a visual layout of events as they are to be seen through the camera lens. And in the case of interactive media, it is the layout and sequence in which the user or viewer sees the content or information. In the storyboarding process, most technical details involved in crafting a film or interactive media project can be efficiently described either in picture, or in additional text.

  Some live-action film directors, such as Joel and Ethan Coen, used storyboard extensively before taking the pitch to their funders, stating that it helps them get the figure they are looking for since they can show exactly where the money will be used. Alfred Hitchcock's films were strongly believed to have been extensively storyboarded to the finest detail by the majority of commentators over the years, although recent research indicates that this was exaggerated for publicity purposes. Other directors storyboard only certain scenes, or none at all. Animation directors are usually required to storyboard extensively, sometimes in place of writing a script.

- ***Theater***

  A common misconception is that storyboards are not used in theater. They are frequently special tools that directors and playwrights use to understand the layout of the scene. The great Russian theatre practitioner Constantin Stanislavski developed storyboards in his detailed production plans for his Moscow Art Theatre performances (such as of Chekhov's The Seagull in 1898). The German director and dramatist Bertolt Brecht developed detailed storyboards as part of his dramaturgical method of "fabels."

- ***Animatics***

  In animation and special effects work, the storyboarding stage may be followed by simplified mock-ups called "animatics" to give a better idea of how the scene will look and feel with motion and timing. At its simplest, an animatic is a series of still images edited together and displayed in sequence. More commonly, a rough dialogue and/or rough sound track is added to the sequence of still images (usually taken from a storyboard) to test whether the sound and images are working effectively together.

  This allows the animators and directors to work out any screenplay, camera positioning, shot list and timing issues that may exist with the current storyboard. The storyboard and soundtrack are amended if necessary, and a new animatic may be created and reviewed with the director until the storyboard is perfected. Editing the film at the animatic stage can avoid animation of scenes that would be edited out of the film. Animation is usually an expensive process, so there should be a minimum of "deleted scenes" if the film is to be completed within budget.

Often storyboards are animated with simple zooms and pans to simulate camera movement (using non-linear editing software). These animations can be combined with available animatics, sound effects and dialog to create a presentation of how a film could be shot and cut together. Some feature film DVD special features include production animatics.

Animatics are also used by advertising agencies to create inexpensive test commercials. A variation, the "rip-o-matic", is made from scenes of existing movies, television programs or commercials, to simulate the look and feel of the proposed commercial. Rip, in this sense, refers to ripping-off an original work to create a new one.

- ***Photomatic***

  A photomatic is a series of still photographs edited together and presented on screen in a sequence.

  Usually, a voice-over, soundtrack and sound effects are added to the piece to create a presentation to show how a film could be shot and cut together. Increasingly used by advertisers and advertising agencies to research the effectiveness of their proposed storyboard before committing to a 'full up' television advertisement.

  The photomatic is usually a research tool, similar to an animatic, in that it represents the work to a test audience so that the commissioners of the work can gauge its effectiveness.

  Originally, photographs were taken using colour negative film. A selection would be made from contact sheets and prints made. The prints would be placed on a rostrum and recorded to videotape using a standard video camera. Any moves, pans or zooms would have to be made in camera. The captured scenes could then be edited.

Digital photography, web access to stock photography and Non-linear editing programs have had a marked impact on this way of film making also leading to the term 'digimatic'. Images can be shot and edited very quickly to allow important creative decisions to be made 'live'. Photo composite animations can build intricate scenes that would normally be beyond many test film budgets.

The term 'photomatic' is probably derived from 'animatic' or photo-animation.

- ***Comic Books***

  Some writers have used storyboard type drawings (albeit rather sketchy) for their scripting of comic books, often indicating staging of figures, backgrounds and balloon placement with instructions to the artist as needed often scribbled in the margins and the dialogue/captions indicated. John Stanley and Carl Barks (when he was writing stories for the Junior Woodchuck title) are known to have used this style of scripting.

- ***Business***

  Storyboards were adapted from the film industry to business, purportedly by Howard Hughes of Hughes Aircraft. Today they are used by industry for planning ad campaigns, commercials, a proposal or other projects intended to convince or compel to action.

  A "quality storyboard" is a tool to help facilitate the introduction of a quality improvement process into an organisation.

  Design comics are a type of storyboard used to include a customer or other characters into a narrative. Design comics are most often used in designing web sites or illustrating product usage scenarios during design.

- ***Interactive media***

  More recently the term storyboard has been used in the fields of web development, software development and instructional design to present and describe, in written, interactive events as well as audio and motion, particularly on user interfaces and electronic pages.

Benefits

One advantage of using storyboards is that it allows (in film and business) the user to experiment with changes in the storyline to evoke stronger reaction or interest. Flashbacks, for instance, are often the result of sorting storyboards out of chronological order to help build suspense and interest.

The process of visual thinking and planning allows a group of people to brainstorm together, placing their ideas on storyboards and then arranging the storyboards on the wall. This fosters more ideas and generates consensus inside the group.

Creation

Storyboards for films are created in a multiple step process.--They can be created by hand drawing or digitally on the computer.

If drawing by hand, the first step is to create or download a storyboard template. These look much like a blank comic strip, with space for comments and dialogue. Then sketch a "thumbnail" storyboard. Some directors sketch thumbnails directly in the script margins. These storyboards get their name because they are rough sketches not bigger than a thumbnail. For some motion pictures, thumbnail storyboards are sufficient.

However, some filmmakers rely heavily on the storyboarding process. If a director or producer wishes, more detailed and elaborate storyboard images are created. These can be created by professional storyboard artists by hand on paper or digitally by using 2D storyboarding programs. Some software applications even supply a stable of storyboard-specific images making it possible to quickly create shots which express the director's intent for the story. These boards tend to contain more detailed information than thumbnail storyboards and convey more of the mood for the scene. These are then presented to the project's cinematographer who achieves the director's vision.

Finally, if needed, 3D storyboards are created (called 'technical previsualization'). The advantage of 3D storyboards is they show exactly what the film camera will see using the lenses the film camera will use. The disadvantage of 3D is the amount of time it takes to build and construct the shots. 3D storyboards can be constructed using 3D animation programs or digital puppets within 3D programs. Some programs have a collection of low resolution 3D figures which can aid in the process. Some 3D applications allow cinematographers to create "technical" storyboards which are optically-correct shots and frames.

While technical storyboards can be helpful, optically-correct storyboards may limit the director's creativity. In classic motion pictures such as Orson Welles' Citizen Kane and Alfred Hitchcock's North by Northwest, the director created storyboards that were initially thought by cinematographers as to be impossible to film. Such innovative and dramatic shots had "impossible" depth of field and angles where there was "no room for the camera" - at least not until creative solutions were found to achieve the ground-breaking shots that the director had envisioned. It is very important that the director not be limited to what is just "possible" or "normal" to the cinematographer. Technical 3D programs can sometimes help the cinematographer plan what challenges the director has created for them to achieve complex storytelling shots.

◆ ◆ ◆

5

MOTIVATION & IDEAS

What drives us to write? A spiritual desire to create art, or a more prosaic need to pay the bills? Whatever the reason, the act of writing demands discipline, effort, commitment and, perhaps above all, motivation. Motivation is the x factor that drives you to sit in front of the computer and move your fingers every day, no matter how much you hate the thought and no matter how badly things are going. If you lose motivation, writing becomes a chore and before long all those odd jobs that you'd put off for years start getting done.You're only too happy to decorate or mend the shed or wash the car. Daytime television takes on a strange allure.Anything to avoid staring at the damn computer.

Writing a screenplay, whether destined to put an Film-Fare on your mantel or to line a litter tray, requires regular hard work towards goals of self-improvement and sales, and involves careful planning, research and execution. Neglect any of these areas at your peril.The best way to build your confidence and improve as a writer is to plan regularly, research regularly and write regularly. Or, to put it more simply, wise up and adopt a professional attitude. The chief obstacle to motivation is fear: fear of groping around in the dark; fear of not being good enough; fear of embarrassment, defeat, failure. One of the aims of this book is to provide the knowledge you'll need to conquer your fear and motivate yourself, allowing you to write with confidence and produce higher quality material.

Finding Your Voice

The prospects of fortune and success in a glamorous industry certainly provide incentives for screenwriters, but don't become sidetracked from the writer's greatest motivation of all: finding something you just have to say; something that makes you lick your lips in anticipation of booting up the computer every day.

Finding your voice is a tricky concept to explain. It's a combination of saying what you want to say, in the way you want to say it, and developing an ability to say it with an originality and flair that makes the combination special.To succeed, your work needs a consistency of vision and a style of execution that elevates it above the average. It should show you in the best possible light; as a creative artist who is professional enough to learn and employ the craft of screenwriting.

Unfortunately, finding your voice is, like everything else, a process – it doesn't happen spontaneously. Don't be surprised when your first efforts appal you and bear little resemblance to what you want to say, or how. It's that way for most of us.

Don't become demotivated and give up because quality can only be arrived at via quantity. If you realise this, you'll be able to expel your initial garbage and write past it.Remember – nothing good is written, it's always *re*written.

Another obstacle is that the prospect of revealing one's innermost idiosyncrasies is often acutely embarrassing. But it is precisely this quality that the industry is looking for – a new voice with something different to say, and a fresh, individual way of saying it. Far too many writers hide their real voices behind façades of structure and plot, leaving their work empty and formulaic.Write your individuality onto the page.

Art vs. Craft

It's dangerous for a screenwriter to view himself solely as an artist. A talented student once told me,"I don't need to learn structure – I want to write a film, not a movie." He never completed a first draft. If you share this highbrow self-image, maybe you should consider other forms of expression: painting, sculpture, novels or poetry. I'm certainly not denigrating such endeavours, but screenwriting is a synergy of craft and art, in that order. It allows plenty of room for creativity – within the parameters of a flexible structure and inflexible format. First learn the craft and then supply the talent because (unless you are truly exceptional) without the artifice, the art will not be enough.

Discipline

If your embryonic writing projects are legion, all once promising but now discarded, or you make good progress until you reach the final straight, you are fleeing the most basic discipline of writing – Finish What You Start. For most of us the reality is that little comes easily. Hard work, hard thought and hard choices are the order of the day, every day. To break through this mental barrier you must develop a disciplined approach that treats writing as the bedrock of your daily life.

One obstacle is that writing sometimes doesn't really feel like work. It's so easy to duck out of.You're at home so you can watch TV, get a sandwich, send emails, whatever. Train yourself to treat writing as a *job*. If you can't write at home,find office space. If you have a full-time occupation, then writing becomes your part-time one. If you don't, then write nine-tofive, or if you're a night owl, nine pm to five am.You alone can decide how much time you can afford.Tuck the writing in comfortably around your commitments, or vice-versa. But be prepared for the possibility that if you simply can't spare enough time and/or energy, or after months you'd still rather have an enema than turn on the computer then, like anything in life, if you can't enjoy it you'd probably be better off doing something else. As Quentin Crisp put it, "If at first you don't succeed, then darling, failure may be your forte."

Routine

Art Arthurs' phrase "Seat of the pants to the seat of the chair" is one of the most motivating mantras I know. I often say it aloud when I'm tempted back to the TV, DVD or CD; it reminds me that the only way to finish what I start is to sit and graft every day. Also, I find writing so much easier when I exercise my brain regularly.

It's all about routine. Discipline demands it and deadlines dictate it. In any job, people prefer to know in advance what they're expected to produce, and when. You should determine your own preferred routine once you've discovered your most productive writing time. When establishing a routine, short-term goal setting is important. Without goals it is far easier to procrastinate, avoid or flee. Goals should be achievable without pushing yourself too hard.

When you're ready to write your first feature script draft, five pages a day will see it completed in around twenty working days. When put like that it somehow doesn't appear as daunting, does it? Just remember that it takes months of research and preparation to reach the draft stage.

One final point: it is important that if there are significant others in your life; partner, children etc, you should discuss your ambitions and your proposed routine with them, and make sure they understand that this is your private time and that you are deadly serious about it. If they are not with you on this it will cause problems. Weigh up the pros and cons. If your activities are reasonable, then go for it – if you don't do it now, you'll probably never do it.

For Whom Do You Write?

Something that comes as a revelation to many students is the concept that you write not for an audience, or the director, or yourself but for the *reader*. Not only a script reader working for a production company but any reader that sits down with your screenplay at any time. People who turn to scriptwriting under the mistaken assumption that it is an easier literary form to master or to sell than a novel couldn't be more wrong. The attraction is easy to see: novels run to hundreds of pages, while screenplay length is 90-120 pages.

Novels maximise, screenplays minimise. Novels tell stories through language, screenplays through visuals. However, the principle of learning the form before trying to produce your best work in it remains the same.You should write with a potential audience in mind but your words must succeed in their own right; they must come alive on the page and entertain anyone who reads them.The fruit of any labour must be of the highest quality to succeed in its market place.

Script Readers

Once you submit your screenplay to production companies, it enters the domain of those mythical industry gatekeepers, the script readers.Their role is to provide written 'coverage' of your script. In *The Guerilla Film Makers Handbook*, a script reader describes the content of coverage: ". . . a brief 'logline' which sums up what the script is about in two or three sentences, a 'synopsis' of what happens in the script, . . . a 'comment' outlining what the script reader feels the script is trying to do, how well it does it, whether the premise is original and engaging, what could be done to improve it and the sort of audience it is likely to appeal to . . . Finally, a 'verdict' or 'recommendation' on the script will indicate whether it should be accepted, rejected or developed."

Readers' instincts are to find reasons to keep the writer out, for which they are often viewed with suspicion or hostility, but their instincts are based on experience – that this script, like the previous one and the one before that, will contain a host of deficiencies from the same predictable menu. Writers load their scripts with them, making the readers' job easy. Do all you can to ensure your script is dramatic, tense, funny, harrowing, touching, entertaining, emotional, *different*; the best art you can produce after researching the craft and the market. Razzle dazzle 'em – if you can make the gatekeepers laugh and cry, the doors to the inner sanctum will start to open for you.

The Value Of Ideas

Ideas are your lifeblood.Without them, your writing will be of little interest to you or to anyone else. They can appear from out of the blue, day or night, and you must be prepared to capture, nurture and develop them. If you can do this, they become your best friends. To update the old Bollywood axiom, ideas are a dime a dozen – and then factor in depreciation. It's always what you do with them that counts and that comes down to talent. If you're a great writer but your ideas are lousy, your script will be lousy, but you can find material to adapt. If your ideas are great but you're a lousy writer, your script will be lousy also, and you should consider collaborating with a good writer. Only if you can transform your best ideas into a marketable commodity – a screenplay that is your very best work, contains originality and style, entertains the reader, is carefully structured, features three-dimensional characters, memorable dialogue, is professionally presented using correct format and binding, with correct spelling, grammar and punctuation – then and only then does the prospect of financial reward enter the equation.

Every writer has different interests, likes and dislikes, and each should play to his own personality. Famus director Subhash Ghai said " . . . 20% of my material is autobiographical, 20% comes from newspapers, 20% from people I know and 20% is pure fiction. Fiction does not play a major part. I prefer to work from real life."

Inspiration

'5% inspiration, 95% perspiration' is a tired catchphrase . . . and also true. Inspiration is vital because without the 5%, the 95% cannot happen.You should cultivate a mindset receptive to inspiration by planning properly, researching thoroughly and writing regularly, thereby reducing your emotional stress and allowing you to think clearly.The more relaxed you are, the more inspired your ideas will become. Don't expect miracles.Your fingers will seldom fly across the keys, spinning reams of golden words.

Mostly, the order of the day is hard work, frustration, anger and self-doubt. Expect to spin 95% manure at first.Your persistence will afford you access to those moments of clarity and excitement more often, the intervals between moments of inspiration will become shorter and the moments themselves will elongate.

Generating Ideas

Like every part of the writing process, this is both discipline and duty. You have to train your mind to think visually, produce ideas in quantity, hold on to inspiration when it strikes, and search all your darkest, dankest corners.

- **Just write.** Stream of consciousness, whatever comes out of your mind. Fill the pages. Any writing process involves reducing quantity to quality.

- **Always have your antenna twitching.** Be receptive to conversations; your own and other people's. It may look strange to someone if you take notes of interesting things they say, but it's better than forgetting them, which you nearly always will.

- **Your own life.**Your experiences are a mine of story ideas, as long as you place them in a dramatic framework and don't expect anyone to be interested in them simply because they're true. As William Goldman wrote, 'Avoid reality.' Reality is mostly uneventful and does not conform to the rules of narrative.

- **Other people's lives.** Look for individual quirks or traits in people you meet. Model a character on a friend (or enemy) or combine elements of several people into one.

- **Invent two skeleton characters, known only by profession.** Give each a singular trait, then give them a reason for meeting, a place for them to meet and an incident to set up or respond to. In other words, something happens to someone, somewhere.You now have a scene, to which you can connect other scenes and other characters.

- **Scan news items on TV/radio and articles in newspapers/ magazines.**Truth is often stranger than fiction, so jot down things that intrigue you and rework them later, or try to incorporate them into other scenarios. Cut out items and keep them in a file, but include a few notes of your first impressions to recapture your interest later. Focus on the universality of these ideas – the essence of their emotional appeal to an audience – because alone they won't amount to much, and if they're too personal to you they may not connect with others.

• **Relax.** Close your eyes. Clear your mind and let your imagination drift, without external stimulus or pressure to create. After about an hour, make notes of the images, sounds and feelings you experienced (in that order), and use them as potential jumping-off points.They may be very strange and make little sense, but they do reveal some of your deepest concerns.

• **Dreams.** Again, don't expect logic or linearity, but do use their excess. Dreams are wonderful for conjuring juxtapositions – two or more incongruous elements placed in a surreal connection. Some of my best dreams have included such startling imagery that I've been unable to forget them. Nightmares are better still – what frightens you is likely to frighten others. And, yes, always write them down.Watch

• **Adapt or 'borrow.'** If you have a favourite novel or play to which you think you could add something, contact the publisher and enquire about the rights.They may be easier and cheaper to secure than you think. Do not adapt as an academic exercise, you'll only make it worse (example: Scorsese's histrionic remake of the excellent *Cape Fear*). Alternatively, rework or update popular works in the public domain – *Clueless* is Jane Austen's *Emma*, *Cruel Intentions* is Choderlos De Laclos' *Les Liaisons Dangereuses*, both updated to contemporary USA.

Capturing Ideas

Always have an ideas pad near you. Keep one by the phone, by the bed, in your study and on your person wherever you go. If something stimulates you; a phone conversation, an overheard anecdote, mental meanderings on a train journey, a news item, an insight into something you're working on – whatever, wherever, whenever – always write it down.

Our best ideas often hit us when we're least able to process them; at the point of sleep.The discipline is to shake yourself awake, flick on the bedside lamp, take an ideas pad and (working) pen from the bedside table and quickly capture the idea and its flavour, i.e. what you love about it.

Ideas & Marketing

The time to identify a market for your ideas is way back at the beginning – if you can't, then neither will others. That said, you should still ask yourself a couple of crucial questions about your central premise:

1. Does it have a realistic chance of selling? If the answer's yes, then:

2. Am I sufficiently in love with it to put my heart and soul into it for six to nine months of my life? If the answer's yes again, then do it; if no, then find something else. If the answer to Q1 is no, Q2 remains the same.Your idea might seem completely uncommercial but if it makes you do cartwheels, then stay with it. If your idea has commercial legs but leaves you cold, your script will be lukewarm at best.You have to be fired up about it to make it hot.

If you want to write character-based, dialogue-driven intimate drama, you should be aware that it is unlikely to sell to the feature film market. If you want to write big-budget, widescreen, fast-moving action thrillers, then your work probably won't interest the TV market. Part of marketing involves building knowledge about the requirements of the industry. Reading this book forms one small part of that process.

◆ ◆ ◆

6

RESEARCH & DEVELOPMENT

Novice writers often make the fatal mistake of neglecting research. It's not only about authenticity (e.g. learning the minutiae of criminal investigation procedure for a police thriller, or comprehensive details of Mumbai Terror Atteck). It also means learning about the film industry and the market place; the great food chain in which you will be competing with thousands of others for scraps. Research is the pursuit of any knowledge that will help you keep up with, or get ahead of, the game – and it never stops.

A significant percentage of students arriving at any screenwriting class confess to almost never visiting the cinema, or never reading scripts, books or magazines about the film industry. It is vital to build an understanding of the industry and the ways in which it operates, and cultivate an informed opinion on what you think works or doesn't work about each film you see and each script you read. You wouldn't apply for a job in an industry you have no knowledge of, so don't expect to write a good script without thoroughly researching the industry and the market, and developing an objective ability to sift diamonds from manure. The more aware you are of the rules, the better your chance of success, whether you use them as a template or a point of departure. When you take your first step toward writing a spec screenplay, you become a self-employed manufacturer. If you don't quickly learn to think like one, your product will never sell. **R & D** – the more thorough your research, the greater your development.

Know Your Market

If you intend to write for film or television, immerse yourself in those media.Watch plenty of films and programmes, but in an analytical capacity.You are no longer a consumer of moving images.Your desire to write scripts propels you from passivity to activity, and you must comfortably exist on an active plane. Expose yourself to a variety of material that reflects the diversity of today's market place. The wider the range of films/programmes you normally watch, the less work you will have to do. If you only like horror or Action or soaps or police dramas, your myopia will cost you.Familiarise yourself with products of different genres and analyse what makes them tick. This common sense imperative often fazes people, perhaps because they aren't used to the concept of personal study outside of academic environments. It's something you need to do if you have a serious ambition to sell your work.

How will you know whether your script stands a chance if you have no knowledge of the market or its demands? How will you know what to include or to avoid in your script? Or to whom it should be sent and how? Or how it should be formatted? Or what font to use? There are hundreds of elements you need to get right when courting the industry. Sending out an unfinished script containing mistakes of structure, layout and presentation, including typographical and grammatical errors, immediately flags you as unprofessional. Even if you later correct these mistakes, you may find it much harder to progress because of the damage your first efforts have caused.

Research Tools

Media products are everywhere; we're bombarded by them on a daily basis. Accessing the means for your research is not difficult. The following list contains thc major products and activities you should pursue to maximise your knowledge, and therefore your chances.

- **Films/TV programmes:** Watch and analyse as many as possible. Concentrate on what you like and dislike; what elements work for you or don't, and always try to explain why. If you like it, exactly what was it that you liked? If you didn't, how would you do it differently? Treat this as a selfstudy programme. Narrow your focus to specific areas like character, dialogue, structure etc.

• **Videos/DVDs:** As above. Many DVDs contain valuable extras including behind-the-scenes documentaries, screenplays, commentaries, Internet links etc.

• **Screenwriting literature:** Read a selection of these books! They are vitally important in achieving a comprehensive understanding of the medium. I highly recommend titles in **hindi-** by Manohar Shyam Joshi, Vinod Tiwari, Rajendra Pandey, in **english-** Ken Dancyger & Jeff Rush, Michael Hauge and Elliot Grove.

• **Film books:** There are many excellent books about the film industry which will build your background knowledge and entertain you at the same time.

• **Trade magazines:** *Screen International* (film, weekly); *Broadcast* (TV, weekly). *Variety* (film, weekly); *Bollywood Reporter* (film/TV, daily).

• **Screenwriting magazines:** Including *Creative Screenwriting*, *Scr(i)pt*, *Scenario*, *Scriptwriter*.

• **Film and related magazines:** Including *Film-Fare*, *Sight & Sound*, *Total Film*, *Uncut*, *Filmi Dunia*.

• **Broadsheet newspapers:** For daily film/TV news and reviews.

• **Tabloid newspapers:** For daily film/TV scurrilous gossip.

• **Scripts:** In book form (usually transcripts of the finished film) or better still, from the Internet. Go to www.script-orama. com for screenplays in various stages from first drafts to shooting scripts.

• **Internet:** The www is the best place to look for all things screen-related.There are legions of sites packed with information on the film and TV business: new releases; old classics; screenwriting; software; production companies; professional and amateur organisations; funding bodies; competitions . . . the list is endless.

• **Writers groups:** Joining a writers group is an obvious way of sharing the lonely burden of writing. An atmosphere of encouragement and mutual support, coupled with invaluable feedback on problem solving and quality is an ideal nurturing environment for writers.

• **Screenwriting courses/workshops/script reading services:** ***Senseindia Foundation® Media Research and Education Forum*** a Film production house that endeavors to create awareness of Filmmaking Tool among intellectuals, media experts, social activists and young enthusiastic people. Apart form Film Production Main stream Activity Senseindia desires to promote activities in Art, Culture, and Informal Education in social interest. An organization founded to by Bapu Sarvagod in 1997 when he is was studying in his post gradation in Film Making in Film and TV institute of India. Since 2002 an organization is functioning to make the sensible Filmmakers with social responsibility Taking media as the first venture, Senseindia started 'the one of its kind' activity called "Film Orientation Workshop" and with perfect facilities provided by the W.R.I.C. and J.P. Naik Bhavan of Mumbai University, Kalina Campus, this developed into a regular programme covering all basic and important topics in Film Making, with camera practical and LCD monitoring and clippings to explain the main points.

As an experience of various training programs Senseindia observes that the people in all the sections of society have some thing to express through the Film Language. People from various parts of the world with deferent professional and age background have participated in Film Making Workshop and they have got confidence as Film Maker and the most important feelings as Film Student. The Senseindia Foundation intends to share the most important key Factors with passionate people so that they can find their own path as par connivance. Of course film Making is always a practical stuff, but still the authentic information is always significant for getting " Knowledge" in Film Making so that Senseindia is devotes for the cause of Enlightening people as Film Maker. Basically Film Maker is that person who thinks of an original Idea, who converts it in to Film script, who Direct and produce it in to Film. Film Making is mare a tool that's vary easy to understand but the most important thing is the THOUGHT that has to be applied in the film

In the film workshop aspirant participants can understand The complete process of Film Making.

Website : www.senseindia.net

- The formation of Idea for Film

- Easy methods to convert concept into Script

- Creation of the Characters and situations

- Inner potential Hunt as creative or technical person

- Understanding ways to achieve success as Film Student and Film Maker

- Getting Confidence as Film Maker

• **University courses:** Still very few specialist postgraduate courses in the India, mainly in writing for TV.

The Language Barrier

You should make every effort to learn the complexities of language.Words are the tools of your trade, so if you're unsure about grammar, punctuation and sentence construction, or can't differentiate between nouns, adjectives and verbs, some research is essential.

Development

Research never stops because knowledge equals power. Thoroughness is the key. Always designate time for research alongside your other activities. Visit libraries, interview people, unearth new contacts or information. If you don't learn, you won't earn.

Developing Your Ideas

OK. Let's assume you've found a concept you like and a promising scenario to build around it. You now want to develop it, but what's the next step? Advice – find out about character and structure. Ideas are much easier to develop when they can be situated within a framework, and as you'll see, characters' actions are at the very heart of structure.Then, go back to your idea and arrive at your premise.

Premise

The premise describes what your script is about; the idea or concept at the heart of your story.Try to summarise it in as few words as possible, to tighten your grip on the central concept and memorise it for 'pitching' to interested parties. Form your premise as a question followed by a complication:

- What happens when a frail old man needs to travel 500 miles to visit his seriously ill brother – but his only mode of transport is a tractor-mower? (*The Straight Story*)
- What happens when a Raman pursues his daughter's killers in Goa – and enters the lion's den with absolutely no fear for his own life? (*The Limey*)
- What happens when a music writer is commissioned by *Femina* magazine to go on tour with a famous rock band – but he is only 15 years old? (*Almost Famous*)
- What happens when a psychologist treats a young boy who claims to see dead people – but doesn't realise that he too is dead? (*The Sixth Sense*)

Readers situate themselves in your protagonist's shoes. The

premise for *The Sixth Sense* really asks readers to ponder: "What would happen if *I* didn't know I was dead?" This is why you should relate your premise to the problems/tasks facing your hero.The premise of *The Insider* might be:What happens when a conscientious scientist is forced to choose between exposing corporate corruption and protecting himself and his family? However, this excludes chief protagonist Lowell Bergman, so would be better as:What happens when a TV reporter exposes deadly corruption in the tobacco industry, but his actions place his own job and organisation in jeopardy, and his vital inside informant's life and family in danger?

High Concept & Low Concept

The term 'high concept' now defaults to mean plot-driven, fast-moving action films, but in practice refers to any film with a strong, clear, easily-summarised concept that will find an audience on the strength of its premise alone.The assumption within the industry is, the higher the concept, the easier it is to market:

- If James Bond were married, what would he tell his wife he does for a living? (*True Lies*)
- What if living dinosaurs could be created from fossil DNA? (*Jurassic Park*)
- Would you sleep with Robert Redford for $1 million? (*Indecent Proposal*)
- What if you could live inside John Malkovich's head? (*Being John Malkovich*)

Some titles are their own premise: *Shakespeare In Love, Bad Lieutenant, Mars Attacks!*

Low, or soft, concept films tend to have more characteroriented premises which, as Charlie Harris says, rely more on the quality of the end product to attract an audience, and are therefore more risky to potential financiers. Hollywood studio product leans towards high concept, most British and European product towards low concept. Bear this in mind when targeting your market. Write genres for the US and characters for the UK.

It's pointless to try to market megabudget science fiction scripts in the UK; ditto political dramas raising awkward questions about American foreign policy in the US (unless set in the US, with a pro-US twist.

Pre-writing

The business of film-making progresses through three stages: pre-production (everything that happens before a foot of film is exposed); production (the film shoot); and post-production (editing, audio dubbing, visual effects,music, captioning etc.). Screenwriting also has three stages: pre-draft, draft and redraft. Drafts and redrafts are covered in chapter 9, so let's look at pre-draft:

Once you've chosen your idea and formed your premise, you'll find yourself making copious notes at any hour of day or night.This is the pre-writing stage when your mind works overtime to produce and keep track of a million disparate, nebulous ideas: images, words, characters, relationships, traits, incidents, locations, plots, sub-plots, emotions, themes and styles. If the premise excites you, you'll be enthusiastic and committed, and think of little else. If it doesn't, you'll do anything to avoid writing.

You need to make clear and comprehensive notes because your brain can't cope with the rush of information. These notes are the missing link between ideas and first draft.They will begin coalescing into something that may, with effort and luck, take on dramatic form and substance.Your notes will steadily connect the disparate elements, piece by slow piece. The picture will form; first in black and white, then colour; first in two dimensions, then three.This is the miracle of creation; the genesis of an organism which did not exist before. Once it does exist, capture the story in a one-page synopsis, including all the major events in chronological sequence. Ask yourself a few questions about your story:What type of story is it? How does it relate to existing types? What are the recognised story types?

◆ ◆ ◆

7

STORY CONCEPT

Every story answers the question *What if such and such happened?* Ex: What if a third-rate fighter had a chance to fight the heavyweight champion of the world? (*Rocky*)

Leads to a plot structure (a town terrorized by a shark in *Jaws*, ghosts and demons plaguing New York City in *Ghostbusters*), or to a character or characters (an indestructible cyborg from the future in *The Terminator*, a group of former 60s radicals in *The Big Chill*). You will be looking for a character to best enhance your plot or the plot situation to best bring out your character.

Expressing the Story Concept

A story concept can be expressed in a single sentence: *It is a story about _ (character/subject) who wants to_ (action/ predicate)* (respectively). Can also include a character who wants something visible, even within this sentence.

Finding Story Ideas

To originate story concepts for screenplays, it is almost always necessary to stimulate your own thinking by observing, recording, and reacting to all of the potential material that confronts you everyday, and to use that material as a jumping-off point for your own brainstorming and creativity. Creativity comes and goes, and sometimes needs your kicking to stir it! Go to the following sources for ideas:

Adaptations of books, plays, and short stories – already provides a plot, get rights to the works. Consider these points: Great literature doesn't necessarily mean great cinema. Bad qualities to bring from books: rich, textured writing; lots of interior thoughts;

feelings, and descriptions; an expansive, convoluted plot; and an abundance of symbol and allegory. Good: character and plot; a style, mood, texture, and structure of own. Don't assume because you like it others will to. You must be truer to your screenplay than to your original source. If you must alter or eliminate parts of the original, do it. Be very wary of adapting your own novels and plays.

Contemporary true stories – Consider

- A story isn't necessarily appropriate for adaptation for a docudrama just because it is true.
- A true story is often more effective as a small segment for TV or the like, not for features.
- Be truer to your screenplay than original source. You may have to spice up events and characters while still maintaining the accuracy and details of the true story.

Historical events

All principles for true stories also apply here. When all principle characters in your dramatization are deceased, then there is no need to obtain rights to the story and are probably in the public domain.

The greatest added difficulty with historical adaptations is commercial. It is a big cost in production and audiences generally like to relate to contemporary characters and events. Using a single book as a source for a historical adaptation means you still must obtain rights to do so.

The strongest and most effective historical screenplays are those which involve some contemporary issue, theme, or plot situation placed in a period context.

Often the best use of historical events is as a jumping-off point for a fictional story.

Headlines – from newspapers, magazines, TV, radio. You don't care about facts or details as you will take the matter in the direction you want it.

Personal experience – Most people's experiences are not

at all interesting enough for a movie or can blind you from proper format. Write about situations and emotions with which you're familiar.

Selecting the best story concepts

Select ideas from your records with both commercial and artistic potential. Commercial potential is the ability to convince the people who make movies and TV shows that the movie of a screenplay will result in profits or high ratings; artistic potential means that a screenplay sets out to do something of value and can succeed on its own terms.

Story Concept Checklist

Must-Have:

1. Hero – main character (human, animal, machine, etc) on screen most of time, whose visible motivation drives the plot, and with whom the audience is deeply involved

2. Identification - Reader must identify with hero. Reader must put self in character's shoes, experience emotion through character

3. Motivation – An objective which the hero hopes to achieve by the end of the story by *wanting something*. Drives the plot forward. Examples: finding a treasure, getting the girl, stopping the killer

4. Obstacles – Serious challenges, hurdles, and obstacles in pursuing motivation. Something has to stand in the way of the main character reaching their motivation, there must be conflict.

5. Courage – to overcome obstacles. The hero must be frightened of the obstacles or something must be on stake for the hero. The audience will stick around to find out is your hero finds what they need or it is unresolved.

6. A high concept – story idea and title sufficient enough to draw in audiences

7. Originality and familiarity – something never seen

before. All successful contemporary films draw on situations that have been explored before: disaster movies, gangster movies. Your elements must be different enough to grab an audience. Use from a winner and be ready to defend your idea's familiarity and originality.

8. Second level of sell and subplots. Second level of sell – gives story concept added originality and depth; a second story line, of equal importance to your original story concept, which also involves your hero and a second, equally important visible motivation for your hero. Ex: *E.T.* "alien from outer space" and "boy and his dog" (second sell).

Usually the second sell is love: A married woman fights to lose weight and meets another man and then loses weight as this new man gives her confidence to do so (*A New Beginning*), or better, An alcoholic actress convicted of murder and trying to prove her innocence, the second sell is her wanting a relationship with the excop who helps her (*The Morning After*) .

9. Familiarity of setting – urban or suburban parts of America in the present. Audiences may fail to relate to foreign places and times in foreign countries with no American culture. Some settings may not be contemporary but familiar enough for a screenplay: old west, World War II, and outer space

10. Genres (Categories) – Write movies in selling categories. Difficult categories:

- Musicals – all singing, all dancing
- Westerns
- Period pieces
- Biographies
- Science fiction – special effects requires lots of money
- Horror – Best for independents, studios rarely produce

original horror films

Best Categories:

- Action-adventure
- Suspense-thriller
- Love story
- Comedy
- Drama
- Any combo of these

11. Medium – Choose: feature film, movie for television, series episode, short film

- **Feature films vs. tv movies**: Features are more expensive, more "panoramic," more graphic in regards to sex and violence, less formulaic, more complex: *Dick Tracy*, *Total Recall*. TV films are more narrow-focused, more topical or issue-oriented, and more standardized in length, structure, etc.

12. Cost – The more expensive to make the movie, the more difficult to be expected. 5 Things make screenplays more expensive to film: Big special effects, a huge cast, lots of exotic locations, a period or historical setting, inclement weather.

13. Character growth – Occurs when a character's search for courage results in greater knowledge, maturation, or actualization.

14. Theme – Universal statement the screenplay makes about the human condition; that which an audience member can apply to their own life. The message is a more political statement that connects directly to the plot and no application to the average person's actions.

Artistry vs. Commerciality

Write movies people want to see. **Checklist to determine if story has a combo of artistry andcommerciality**

1. Do I want to spend at least the next six months of my life working on the story idea?

2. Does this story have commercial potential?

3. If no, do you have the passion to see to it is written? Consider:

• Writing should be personal fulfilling.

• Most screenplays don't get sold anyway but serve as a sample of your work

• If you do a good enough job from passion, eventually it'd get sold.

Modifying Story Concept

1. If the concept is not provocative enough, can you add other elements to give it more immediate interest and a higher concept?

2. Can you combine the initial concept with another idea to give it a second level of sell or additional subplots?

3. If the setting isn't particularly familiar, could it be changed to contemporary America without destroying the other aspects of the story?

4. If the story is similar to other films, can you create elements that will add originality to thc familiarity of the concept?

5. If the cost of filming the story seems prohibitively high, can the cost be lowered by changing the location or the period or by reducing the number of secondary characters?

◆ ◆ ◆

8

"My Movie" Story Development

8 Essential Elements:

- **CONFLICT** - The struggles and obstacles
- **PLOT** - The events and action
- **SETTING** - The world of the story; time/place
- **STRUCTURE** - The combination of all the elements
- **THEME** - The controlling idea
- **MOOD/ATMOSPHERE** - The tone or feel
- **POV**- The character we mainly view the "movie" from.
- **CHARACTERS** - The inhabitants of your story

CHARACTER PROFILES:

Choose to write only what is equivalent for your script. Remember : too specific can cause casting problems!

- NAME :
- Character : hero, nemesis, reflect, major, secondary
- BIOGRAPHY : Past events
- AGE :
- HEIGHT :
- WEIGHT :
- BODY TYPE :
- FACE TYPE :
- COMPLEXION :
- EYES :
- HAIR :

- RELIGION :
- ORIENTATION :
- RACE :
- CLOTHING STYLE :
- SPEAKING STYLE :
- GENERAL DEMEANOR :
- CAREER :
- PREJUDICES :
- BEST QUALITIES :
- WORST QUALITIES :
- WEAKNESSES :
- HOBBIES :
- TALENTS :

BRIEF DESCRIPTION: what goes in your script.

PLOT

Begin by writing a single sentence identifying the main character and what they want or hope to accomplish.

My main character is _ and they want _.

My main character is Jai and he wants to graduate from law school.

Now write a concept, a three sentence structure along the lines of beginning – middle – end.

Jai, a redneck rebel, moves out of his family farm to confront college life. He finally graduates from undergraduate school and heads off to law school. He runs into problems where blossoms his first love.

Now expand each sentence into their own paragraph. You are building the structure of the movie.

◆ ◆ ◆

9

WHAT MAKES A GOOD STORY?

There are many elements that form the construction of a good story. Debatably, a good story is the fundamental aspect of many forms of art, whether it be a novel, a painting, a TV series, a film, a play, poetry, music or even computer games, so it is vital that it has a strong impact.

Story can be divided into many different sections, but I've decided on three major places to analyse briefly - **Character**, **World** and **Plot**. Some people would argue that these have equal importance; some might say one has higher relevance than the next; the fact is all three contribute in some way to the story's overall reception and this article intends to look at major points within each of these.

1. Character

If I were obliged to rate the most important aspect of story from the three options I've stated, I would choose **Character**. However, this is just my opinion and there is plenty of examples out there that prove that, **World** or **Plot** can be the driving force of a story. Still, I feel that a strong character, whether an evil antagonist, a benevolent hero, a confused anti-hero or a reformed criminal is the axis of a good story. But why?

In the classic play *Othello* written by Shakespeare in1603, you had an extremely potent and affective villain, Iago. What made him so strong was the fact that he managed to manipulate every other protagonist in the play without being caught, until his desire for revenge was complete. His successful vengeance confirms his strength as a character and made the whole drama very compelling.

In the more modern *Harry Potter* series, despite the fact that the lead, Harry Potter is considered by some readers as annoying, there are plenty of other characters to choose from throughout the books, each with strengths and weaknesses that a large audience will find some interest in.

One of the most conspicuous ways to show what characters are about is when they bounce off one another to highlight their weaknesses or strengths. A very extreme example I saw recently was in the TV series *Dexter*. This show follows a man who as a child witnessed the horrific murder of his mother. Since this tragedy, the violent nature of the crime rendered the child with no emotions and thus, opened the door to the creation of a serial killer. His foster father, the police officer who rescued him, recognised this character deformation in the child's early years and realised he would have to act to prevent his surrogate son from becoming a mass murderer. Thus, he gave his son a code to live by - only kill the guilty i.e. other predators - rapists, killers e.t.c.

Now, on deeper perception of this, this protagonist is one seriously deranged human being, because he has to kill people in order to keep his blood lust in check, but what makes him different and highlights a twisted form of virtue in him is the other serial killers he confronts.

Their minds are so much worse than his and they have no code to live by. It makes the audience feel comfortable with the protagonist's hobby of killing other serial killers, despite the fact that it's a sick urge that he possesses.

The main reason I find **character** to be so important is that it's that person's perception that you're going to take on when you read the story. If he has dry, boring conceptions, it won't make the story very interesting and even if the **World** or **Plot** are amazing, it would be hard to retain interest in a story if the lead role has no depth or intrigue to him/her.

So little aspects of both their physical appearance or mentality need to be depicted well - it can be that he has a scar on his face or a nervous twitch, but anything to generate questions in the reader's mind about this character's history is always good and improves the story's delivery.

2. World

The invention of the world for the story is a vital point. One of the great aspects to classic writers like Charles Dickens or contemporary writers like Phillip Pullman is their ability to capture the world around them. Now whether this is attempting to portray our world - the human world or some fantastical dimension, painting a convincing picture of that world is key through powerful description and more to the point, vivid imagery.

You want to be able to see the world, hear it, smell it, touch it, taste it - all the senses need to be tingled for the success of this invention and that was one of the most astonishing things about Phillip Pullman's *Dark Materials Trilogy.* He was presenting lots of different universes with bizarre creatures and to do this credibly, he had the arduous task of making you believe these worlds could exist. This writer went as far as to take on the mission of presenting his depiction of God, angels and the heavens. This is one of the hardest things any artist can do in an increasingly atheistic society. Still, judging by the popularity of this series, he clearly accomplished this.

The issue with world is that it's a static phenomenon. That's not to say that it can't be massively animated, but the character is the one who's going to do the moving around. He/she is the one who's going to draw his conclusions from what he sees and he's the one who will affect the world around him. Hence, **World** is relevant to a good story, but I'm convinced that **Character** is the one that breathes life into the tale.

3. Plot

Believe the most important part of **Plot** is suspense. There are plenty of other things in **Plot** like the themes and ideas conveyed; these could be good versus evil, emotion, greed e.t.c. but suspense is what keeps people asking questions and reading on: Why is this character so angry? What happened to this person's wife? Why is this child traumatised?

Through this, **Plot** adds to making a good story, but again I summarise that character is the one driving the plot. **Plot** appears to be something conceived by the characters and what they do. If he/she is attacking someone and you have no idea why - you're asking questions related to their actions. So, in conclusion, I believe a good story comes from the characters, since the other two elements appear to be generated or amplified by the characters themselves.

◆ ◆ ◆

10

UNDERSTANDING STORY & PLOT

To understand the function of story and plot, it is important to distinguish between them.Many people refer to one when they mean the other. The difference is a simple, but crucial, one:

Story – all of the elements contained within the narrative, in chronological order. In other words, everything that happens to all of the characters placed in a straight line through time.

Plot – how the writer chooses to order the story elements; intercutting main plots and sub-plots, and incorporating flashbacks, flashforwards etc. if necessary.

STORY, CHARACTER, INCIDENT, STRUCTURE

After our genre digression, let's get straight back to your story.Your premise is exciting and your notes are progressing at a furious rate.At this stage you'll be thinking in story terms – beginning, middle, end – when developing your material, but the problem of how to organise the plot will constantly nag at the back of your mind. Keep it there for now. Only begin plotting when you have all of your main story events and you're ready to sequence them.

Don't be tempted to construct your events too skeletally and neglect the key ingredients of your story – characters and incidents.The narrative world can't exist without them, they are inextricably intertwined. If you treat the story development as an academic exercise, even in a whodunnit mystery, your work will be sterile and airless, and your characters won't be able to breathe. The mechanics of cause and effect are always secondary to inventing and communicating a living world with a consistent set of rules.The world of your story should feel as realistic to readers as their own, and your characters must be equally realistic to live there.

STORY is formed by characters' actions as they cause or react to incidents, overcome obstacles and pursue goals.

CHARACTERS cannot act without goals to strive for, problems to overcome and incidents to respond to.

INCIDENTS need to be seen from the perspective of their effects on characters' lives, to give readers a human element with which to identify.

STRUCTURE is the framework which supports the story and supplies the most drama, conflict and tension to draw readers in and maintain their emotional involvement.

The story world (macrocosm) must be presented through characters and incidents (microcosm). Even in a large-scale genre thriller like *Heat*, the cops-and-robbers macrocosm is boiled down to the Vincent Hanna versus Neil McCauley microcosm. The bravura daylight set pieces would have far less impact without examining each character's specific behavioural attitudes to them before, during and after.

Theme

When pitching your project to someone important, don't be surprised if, after you tell them the premise, they say "Okay – but what's it *really* about?" What they're asking for is the theme.They're also asking whether or not *you* know it. If you don't, there's an old Hollywood maxim that goes, "If your script is about what it's about, you're in deep shit."

Your script must be about more than it appears to be on the surface. Not only in terms of plot and sub-plot, but also theme.The theme is the expression of the universal value of your story; the reason why it will connect with an audience. It may not arrive in your mind until your script is finished, but it will spring from what motivated you to write your script in the first place.What they are actually asking you is "What do you really want to *say*?"Theme can be expressed in one word (revenge, integrity, greed, justice), but this doesn't tell anyone much. Something like "The amazing ability of the human spirit to triumph over adversity, or against the odds" is better, but you'll be politely told that most stories fit this description.Try to be specific about your particular theme.

Themes are about emotion.Your primary task as a screenwriter is to convey the emotional impact of your script to a reader.This is one difference between a cinematic and a televisual premise.The cinematic premise may be action or character- oriented, but should connect and resonate with the audience's emotions on a level that a televisual premise cannot. It's not just about exaggeration, it's also about sustaining an emotionally charged narrative for two hours and keeping an audience engaged. After being shot, Andy Warhol said "People sometimes say that the way things happen in the movies is unreal. But actually it's the way things happen to you in life that's unreal.The movies make emotions look so strong and real, whereas when things really do happen to you, it's like watching television.You don't feel anything."

In a great script there may be several themes. One in *Field Of Dreams* is Second Chances: If you were granted another chance to have something that you only realised was important when it was gone, how far would you go to take it? To Ray Frensham, the theme is: "It is important for us to have dreams – even if those dreams are not ultimately fulfilled, it is important for us to have them." Many themes are present because of the skilful layering and essential humanity in Phil Alden Robinson's script.

Conflict & Tension

Syd Field says,"Without conflict there is no drama." Conflict arises from situation, but more importantly from character, and should be present in every scene.The goals and needs of the protagonist meet opposition from without (other characters or situations) and from within (inner demons, conscience, fear, ghosts), creating conflict. Tension builds in the gaps between eruptions of conflict, but is also everpresent in the opposing goals or values of characters. Every major character needs polarities, within themselves and in their relationship to others. Polarities create conflict and tension. Include some form of conflict in every scene: physical, psychological, situational. When you lose sight of conflict, you also lose readers' interest.

Building & Releasing Tension

The opening sequence of Robert Harmon's horror thriller, *The Hitcher*: A young man (C Thomas Howell), exhausted from driving in the rain all night, picks up a soaking hitchhiker (Rutger Hauer) in the middle of nowhere.The young man then runs an incredibly tense gauntlet as the hitch-hiker first refuses to say where he's headed, then sticks a knife in his face and relates in graphic detail how he cut up the last guy who gave him a ride, and tells him he's to meet the same fate unless he can stop him. Finally the young man summons the courage and strength to lunge at the hitch-hiker – who falls out of the door he left ajar. The young man yells and slams the dash in a frenzy of freed tension as the hitch-hiker bounces along the dark, wet road. CUT TO:

INT/EXT. Desert Road – Day.The young man is taking it easy. A station wagon overtakes. Two children in the rear window pretend to shoot him with toy guns. Smiling, he 'shoots' back with his finger, then freezes as slowly, between the two children, arms around their shoulders, rises the hitch-hiker . . . A textbook lesson on the rhythms of tension. Slowly build to a crescendo, then release . . . and immediately start to build again.

Reversing Expectation

You're watching a film.You're thinking "I know what's going to happen next."You experience a slight rush of anticipation. Then, it happens. Exactly as you thought. And you feel . . . disappointed.The slight rush was because you secretly hoped that it *wouldn't* happen; that the film would surprise you, show you something clever and unexpected. I remember watching *Fatal Attraction*, sitting behind two old ladies who kept whispering to each other what they thought would happen next. Normally this would incur my wrath, but this time I kept quiet and listened – and they were right, every time, because they found the film's reversals and switches so predictable.

Try to subvert expectations of genre as well as story.

When developing your story, ask yourself what you would expect to happen next if this were someone else's script – and then don't do it. Reverse it. As often as possible. If you can place a few major and several minor reversals in your script, that readers won't see coming, then you'll keep them turning the pages. It's about uncertainty, and the building of suspense. If you also reverse the tone, then even better.

Ellipsis

Simply, cutting out the dead time. Real life consists of millions of dull moments interspersed with a few vital, dramatic ones – if you could tune in to Tom Cruise's life for days on end, you would be mostly bored to tears. Story world and real world are in fact worlds apart. In *The Truman Show*, Truman Burbank's every waking hour is manipulated in an artificial environment for a unique TV show. Once he becomes aware of this, he has to escape the cloying story world and gain his freedom. Similarly, in *EdTV*, the TV execs realise that Ed's life just isn't interesting enough to the viewers without dramatic intervention. Screenwriting excises the boring 'real world' moments and gives characters a series of vital, dramatic situations compressed into a narrative framework. Ellipsis allows these events to appear connected and seamless, almost as though they were playing out in real time.

Screen Time & Narrative Time

Screen time is the duration of the film; usually 11D 2–2 hours, based on the average audience's attention span. Narrative time is the duration of the story events.This can be real time (*High Noon*'s narrative clock begins ticking at 10:30 am; the showdown is at, er, noon), decades (in *Back To The Future* and *Pleasantville*, the protagonists are displaced from the present to the 1950s), or several millennia (*2001:A Space Odyssey* moves from the Dawn of Man to a space mission to Jupiter). A tip: if you're writing for a low-budget independent market, compress your script's narrative time into weeks rather than months, days rather than weeks.Try not to include exterior locations showing seasonal changes – it's too expensive.

Start At The End

The earlier you know your climax/finale/dénouement, the easier the writing process becomes. If you are secure in the knowledge that you have a satisfying resolution, your confidence will be greater. On a more practical level, you can write 'backwards,' setting in place everything that narrows focus to your climax, rather than writing reams of exploratory material in the hope that it will lead to a tight and exciting conclusion.

Great Scenes

When the memory of a film has faded into a blur, the great scenes are the ones people remember.You'll be able to recall dozens of your own favourites without too much thought. Every script should contain a handful of scenes that provide memorable, standout moments where the reader thinks "Wow, I wish I'd written that!" If one of your script's great moments is its climax, you're ahead of the game.You'll know them by the time you come to write the first draft.They'll be the scenes that set your pulse racing; exciting, vital, inspired and almost fully-formed in your mind's eye.You're itching to see them in the movie and you can visualise them down to the smallest detail.

In *The Double Life Of Véronique* there are four beautiful set piece scenes: the first is in the square during the demonstration when Veronika is trying to collect her spilled sheet music, then watches in awe as her identical double is herded back on board a French tour coach; the second is Veronika's tragic concert début; the third is the poignant puppet show at the junior school where Véronique teaches music; and the fourth is the café meeting when the puppet master reveals the devastating reason why he has been sending her 'clues' to bring her to this place at this time.

PLOT

Once your major story events are laid out in chronological form, you can move on to the complexities of plotting. As Jean-Luc

Godard said, "A film should have a beginning, a middle and an end, but not necessarily in that order."

Plots may or may not follow a linear progression. In *Pulp Fiction*, the first story event occurs when the young Butch is given his dead father's gold watch by one of his army colleagues, but this event is placed an hour into the plot. *Citizen Kane* opens with the death of Charles Foster Kane, and the plot then flashes backwards and forwards, piecing together a jigsaw of Kane's character by relating key events from his life as witnessed by those closest to him. In *Memento*, the narrative again begins with the last story event, then runs backwards in short overlapping segments, the plot structure cleverly paralleling the protagonist Leonard's ten-minute memory span. *The Limey* is a patchwork quilt of fleeting non-sequential images which layer together to form a complex emotional mood.

Before you order your plot events, you should have five fixed points established in your mind: opening sequence, climax/resolution, two end of act watershed incidents (plot points) and your mid-point. The art of plotting revolves around trying to find the most effective dramatic structure for your story. See chapter 6 for ways in which plot and structure intertwine.

Main Plot

The main plot follows the protagonist's action line through the story. It connects with his outer motivations and the obstacles he faces.The main plot forms the immediate foreground of the narrative and carries the major thrust: to get the hero from the inciting incident to his goal in around one hundred pages.

Sub-Plots

Sub-plots involve other characters and events that connect directly or indirectly to the protagonist's main plot.The foremost sub-plot reveals the protagonist's inner struggle to conquer those elements within himself that stand in his way. Other characters and events may be connected to each other, but they are all somehow connected to the protagonist and his actions. They may run parallel to the main plot, or contrary to it. Cutting to sub-plots is a way to create anticipation in the reader by delaying the resolution of elements or tensions in the main plot. Sub-plots are also useful carriers of theme.The protagonist's main plot is usually concerned with his actions to solve problems, complete tasks or achieve goals, but the theme that resonates with an audience may concern a sub-plot involving romance or injustice or hardship or anything that conveys the true emotion of your story.

Exposition

The reader needs to be provided with information about the context of your script; the background to the events of the plot. In a science fiction story set in the future or on a distant planet, you will need to inform the reader how the world evolved from the world we're familiar with, or what particular conditions exist in this alien environment. Obviously you don't have time or space to supply a full future history, but you must supply the information relevant to the story. This is known as setting your exposition, and applies to characters as well as events.Your characters have lived lives which have brought them to their start point and set up their individual and collective narratives. Events in their recent past will particularly influence who and how they are when readers first encounter them. As Lajos Egri said,"Motivation must have grown out of what happened *before* the story started.Your story is *possible only because it grew out of the very thing that happened before.*" How you choose to relate these significant 'backstories' will require a lot of thought, and may result in shifts along your narrative timeline. Voice-overs, flashbacks, flashforwards etc. are satisfying plot devices when well-crafted, but for a novice screenwriter they present problems of complexity and are often badly executed.The characters cannot tell their own stories; you must show the relevant events and incorporate them into your plot. You must also do this quickly; readers need to know what's going on and why, as soon as it happens. Most, if not all, of your expository detail should be placed in Act I, to set up the complications that occur in Act II.

That said, holding back a crucial element of exposition can maximise readers' anticipation. In *Jaws*, a Great White shark is cruising around Amity Island, killing swimmers and ruining the tourist trade. Three disparate individuals join forces to hunt it. Chief Brody has a big city background and doesn't even like water. Hooper is an ambitious but unproven marine biologist. Quint is an enigma because his backstory is deliberately delayed. He's driven, abrasive and opinionated, but his past is an unknown quantity. He is the focus of the tensions between the three men as they hunt the killer shark, and of the crucial 'drinking' scene after the shark first gets away. This memorable scene is multifunctional; it solves the problem of how to bond the men together to function as a unit, and culminates in Quint's superb 'USS Indianapolis' monologue which finally delivers his backstory (worth the wait), establishes his credentials, clarifies his motivation to kill the shark and brings the difficulty of their task into sharp relief.

Exercise: Watch one of your favourite films and write down a brief

11

CHARACTER DEVELOPMENT

It is through the characters your reader will experience emotion. The three facets of character :

- **Physical makeup**: age, sex, appearance, disabilities
- **Personality**: intelligence, emotional makeup, etc.
- **Background**: everything that happened to the character prior to his appearance in the screenplay.

Developing Your Hero

To create the hero which bests suits your story plot, determine those qualities the character should possess to suit the logic and reality of basic plot. Create the necessary identification with the hero for the reader. Must add those individual facets to the character to make him or her original and provocative.

Create a Rough Outline of Your Hero

If you have no idea about your characters, follow these steps:

- What limits are placed on this character by the plot situation itself? Must the character possess a certain age, sex, background, level of intelligence, or personality?
- Using thc sourccs from chapter 2 (headlines, etc.), as a stimuli for character traits for your hero. Brainstorm rather than edit; keep an open mind before narrowing traits.
- Research the area of your story concept. Observing, interviewing, and researching can help.

Establish Character Identification

The audience and reader must identify with the hero of the story. These principles must be used for main character but can be used for other ones:

- **Sympathy** – give audience a reason to feel sorry for the character by being victim of misfortune; sooner deployed the better
- **Jeopardy** – Get reader to worry about character by putting them in dangerous situation, examples: threat of capture, exposure, embarrassment, or defeat
- **Likeable** – Get reader to like character: at least 1 or combo of 3 ways:

1. Make the character a good or nice person.

2. Make the character funny.

3. Make the characters good at what they do.

- **Immediate introduction** – First ten minutes; the audience awaits for someone to identify and root for
- **Possession of power** – 3 forms: 1. Power over other people 2. Power to whatever needs to be done, without hesitation no matter what stands in their way 3. Power to express one's feelings despite opinions.
- **A familiar setting** – Even if it's something people have heard but may not themselves experience
- **Familiar flaws and foibles** – Undeserved misfortune and a funny character, respectively.

Specific only to certain kinds of films:

- **An archetypal superhero** – such as Superman, James Bond. We present emotion through their similarity to heroes of myths, legends, and fairy tales
- **The eyes of the audience** – The audience learns information only when the hero does from someone observing the hero, or create identification with one character and transfer to another.

Make Your Characters Original

Research subject area (if about firefighters, talk to real firefighters). Go against cliché by altering the physical makeup, background, and personality – For a cop, don't go with a white strong guy but the opposite. Change all traits given to character to their opposite (still brainstorming, so quality not quantity). Ex: *Columbo* and many characters in *Police Academy.* Pair with opposite character – Brings out more ideas, ex: Punky Brewster and James Bond. Cast the character – Imagine a certain actor playing the part and create the character around them. Use other actors as well for well-roundedness – never mention names.

Motivation

What the character hopes to achieve by end of movie; Specific way any character, mostly hero, determines plot – the one-line sentence from Story Concept. What hero desires determines what story is about: *Ghostbusters* – story about a former university teacher who wants to earn money by getting rid of ghosts.

Two levels: Outer and inner

Outer: What the character visibly hopes to accomplish by the end of the movie; drives plot of story and determines basic story concept (mandatory)

Inner: The reason (why?) for the outer motivation, which the character thinks will lead to self-worth (optional)

: : Comparisons : :

Outer	**Inner**
Visible	Invisible
Desire for outward accomplishment	Desire for self worth
Revealed through action	Revealed through dialogue
Answers question: What this?	Answers question, Why does he want to do
Is this movie about?	
Related to plot	Related to character growth and theme

Reasons for accomplishing a task (work, school, etc) differs per person as in real life. Paths of self-worth: revenge, greed, power

Conflict

Is whatever stands in the way from the hero achieving his goal; sum of all hurdles and obstacles to reach objective

The sources of conflict are:

Outer – Nature or other characters

Inner – Within the character

Developing the Other Characters of Your Screenplay

Primary Characters

You will be in one of these two situations:

1. You may already have a cast of characters in mind, you're adapting a story, the logic of the plot dictates certain character types. Characters will function effectively if you know the basic function each fills in relation to hero

2. May have your hero worked out but have no idea who the other characters in the story will be. Knowing the basic categories is then helpful because you know you must originate people for your story who will fulfill specific functions (Using *A Nightmare on Elm Street* as example):

Four Basic Categories of Primary Characters

1. **Hero** - Main character, whose outer motivation drives plot forward, primary object and on screen most of time. Must possess some outer conflict and motivation (Nancy)

2. **Nemesis** – Character who stands in the way of the hero achieving his or her outer motivation; a villain, opponent, or good guy (Freddy Krueger)

3. **Reflection** – character who supports the hero's outer motivation (her father) or at least some basic situation at the beginning of the screenplay. Can be friend, co-worker, sidekick, spouse, mate, lover, etc. Create reflection characters because it adds credibility to your

plot if your hero has help in overcoming the outer conflict, it gives the hero someone to talk to, making it easier to reveal background, inner motivation, inner conflict, and theme or to create anticipation

4. **Romance** – character who is the sexual or romantic object of at least the hero's outer motivation, and must always support such motivation (her boyfriend). Audience must fall in love or understand with character as well if hero does so.

Rules for Creating Primary Characters

1. Characters must be people unless human or humanoid; not an animal, situation, or force of nature
2. Inner motivation and conflict may or may not be explored for any of the primary characters. Usually done so for the hero, if at all
3. It is not necessary to have a character in each category. Hero and at least one other categories a MUST. All depends on your story.
4. A character cannot fall into more than one category.
5. A character cannot change categories. Defined by the way they function at the beginning of the film or first introduced. Audiences ask themselves:

    a. Who am I rooting for and what do they want? (hero and motivation)

    b. Who is shc up against (nemesis)

    c. Who is going to help her (reflection)

    d. Who will she fall in love with (romance)

6. It is possible to have more than one charactcr in any of the categories. Duel and multiple heroes occur frequently (Nancy, her father) For new writers, stick to only single categories.

Rules When Creating Nemesis:

1. Good villains make good movies – the stronger and more formidable, the better the story.
2. Must be visible and specific character, not a collective

noun ("Mafia"), force of nature ("cancer") or quality of life ("evil in the world"). If coming up against government, terrorists, etc., then use a specific character from these groups as nemesis. Does not mean audience must know nemesis identity.

3. Must show the final confrontation between your hero and nemesis (most of time the climax – point hero succeeds or fails to achieve outer motivation)

Secondary Characters

Are all the other people in your screenplay, the characters you create to add logic, humor, complexity, texture, depth, and reality to your screenplay after delineating your primary characters. Let these characters serves as many of the previous stated functions but employ them in terms of your hero's outer motivations so not to confuse the plot. Create them on an as needed basis for a perfect balance of character development.

Charting Character, Motivation, and Conflict

Characters		**O Motivation**	**O Conflict**	**I Motivation**	**I Conflict**
Hero	Nancy	To Live	Fred Krueger	N/A	N/A
Nemesis	Fred Krueger	Seek revenge	Teens playing with him	He's pissed off	N/A
Reflection	Father	To help his daughter	Society	He loves her	N/A
Romance	Boyfriend	To live	Wanted for murder he didn't commit	He loves her	Fear of being found guilty

Theme

Theme is universal; it applies to everyone about human condition. It grows out of plot ONLY. Wait until a few drafts before you define it. Themes are optional. It is a prescription to how one should live one's life in order to be more fulfilled, more evolved, or a better person (morality)

Theme emerges when the hero's similarity to the nemesis and difference from the reflection are revealed.

There is something inside motivating you to write, something you want to say. This is the movie message, called theme. Don't focus on the theme. The resolution will verify the acceptability of your message. It's something you've been wanting to say – the point of view of your story. CHINATOWN theme: You can get away with murder if you have enough money. The theme is the writer's view of how people should act in the world. Theme is what your movie is about, one thing, a theme or idea, and every scene and character is formed from the fountainhead. New stories can also deal with thematic material. In a few stories it may be possible to create a thematic or symbolic character: someone whose purpose is to carry a theme, value, or even story message, seldom the central character: mathematician in JURASSIC PARK.

Theme grows out of the writer's unconscious, is developed through the characters' unconscious, and is received by the audiences' unconscious. Theme must grow out of the story concept; it must never be imposed on it.

Theme is not a message. A message is a political statement which applies to a specific group of people or a specific situation.

Several levels of meaning in exploring themes are possible: symbol, allegory, archetype, etc.

Character growth

Character growth occurs when the hero recognizes her own similarity to the nemesis and difference from the reflection.

Keys to creating captivating characters

A Goal and an Opposition

Your character wants a goal – dramatic is specific and measurable. Dealing with life is not a goal; seeking $10 million worth of a historic artifact is. The nature of a goal reveals a lot about your character.

The goal should not be easy to attain. There must be opposition, which creates conflict, which then makes drama. Conflict reveals character and motivates people to learn. Ask: What does my character want and what does she fear most? Opposition will force her to face her fear.

The opposition should be an individual or an individual representing an organization. EX: GHOSTBUSTERS: The EPA is represented by a man who is after the Ghostbusters.

Where a group opposes the central character, such as a gang, focus on one person in the group who's the greatest threat to that character. Personalizing the opposition creates greater drama and will elicit the audience's sympathy for the central character. The hero is defined by their opposition. It need not be evil, just someone who has a good attempt to block your main character's goal. When choosing a nonhuman opposition, such as nature or monsters (JAWS), consider adding a human opponent as well. A well-written story often features three opponents.

Also give your character some related inner drive or yearning that either supports the goal or is in opposition to it. This need may be inwardly blocked by some character flaw.

Motivation

Your character must be motivated. Ask: Why does my character want what he wants? Answer: motivation. The more personal, the better because the audience will sympathize and identify with more.

Ex: ROCKY

What is Rocky's Goal? Specific; wants to go the distance with the champ – 15 rounds.

Why? To prove he's not a bum.

Such motivation gives the story its power.

Back-story

Before page one, something happens to your character – a back-story, a brief history about a character. Usually, a back-story is not seen by the audience, but is there, haunting the central character and affecting his actions. Sometimes only the writer knows the back-story (AS GOOD AS IT GETS) but this allows the characters to seem fuller. It can be subtle: in STARMAN, Karen Allen's need is to learn to live again now that her husband is dead. Occasionally, the audience is known the back-story. EX: CONTACT opens with the back-story.

The Will to Act

Action reveals character, and crisis reveals his true colors because a person does what he does because of who he is. Problems and obstacles reveals what he's made of. Since actions speak louder than words, your character will generally reveal more through action than dialogue. Dialogue can be action – When Darth Vader tells Luke that he is his father and that he should join him, that's an action.

A Point of View (POV) and Attitudes

Everyone has a belief system, perception of reality influenced by past experience, a point of view developed over time. Two people may react in totally different ways to the same stimulus, dependent upon their perception. Their point of view is expressed in attitudes. Your character has a past. Ask: What is your character's point of view about life? What is your character's concept of love? How does he or she view the opposite sex? What is your character's attitude toward growing old? Sex? Falling rain? Grocery shopping? Dental hygiene and regular professional care? Is happiness a warm puppy or a warm gun? Give each character their own set of facts, different views and beliefs, regardless how that POV squares with reality. When a character's point of view changes, that's character growth.

Room to Grow

Your main character also has a point of view of self, called selfconcept. I'm a winner… all of us act from this point of view and so do your characters. Realization is when the character has realized the change which has taken place.. Usually follows the Showdown (climax) but can take place during or just before Showdown.

EX: WIZARD OF OZ: Dorothy realizes there is no place like home.

Growth comes about through adversity and opposition striving for a goal. Only through conflict, making decisions, and taking actions. Ask yourself how your character learns or grows. Often they will grow from some form of slavery to some form of freedom (TITANIC), but can be from death to life (STARMAN). A character can learn to love (RAINMAN) or overcome pride (DRIVING MISS DAISY) or become more principled (AN AMERICAN PRESIDENT).

In some films, such as action/adventures, thrillers, and others, the main character may not grow. James Bond doesn't grow; he just accomplishes his mission. In most genres character growth is desirable and essential.

Believability

Dramatic characters are interesting usually because they are singleminded and focused. Humans tend to run off on tangents. Make your dramatic and comedic characters seem as human as possible – make us care about them:

- **Give them human emotions**: Allow the audience's emotions to identify with the feelings of your characters. A character is empathized more when she fights what she feels rather than when she expresses it.

- **Give them human traits**: Focus on the core of your character – the soul. Who is she? What is her strongest trait? Look for a flaw that might serve as contrast, to create inner conflict. You don't have to reveal character traits all at once. Each scene should reveal something new about your central character. Each contact with a new character sheds light until the central character is fully illuminated. Introduce your central character in normal circumstances before the catalyst upsets that balance so that we have a feel for whom this person is. This can be done by other characters talking about the central character. Include characteristics, problems, and imperfections that are familiar to all humans – He's a grouch. These will make your dramatic or comedic character more believable and more human. An opposition character's imperfections might be more irritating than enduring You can also determine astrological signs, personality and psychology tests. Get books on these subjects!

• **Give them human values**: Give your characters positive values (such as loyalty and a sense of justice in GODFATHER). Bad guy central characters should be superior morally than others in story. If he breaks the law, make him less corrupt than the law. Give your character a talent for what they do, and/or endearing personal style in how she does it. Give her a moment alone to reveal her goodness. Confront your character with an injustice, or place him in a difficult situation or in jeopardy. Be careful not to make him too much a victim.

• **Give them human dimension**: Your characters should have dimension. Avoid cardboard characters and stereotypes – use depth. No onc is complctely evil or good. The most loved characters in film have depth and dimension (bloodied faces, flaws, etc.).

• **Heroes and villains**: Depending on nature, your character lies somewhere between real life and cartoon. Some heroes are swashbucklers with a hardy flaw, others are bad all the way. Other films go deeper. The hero is often ordinary who becomes a hero on his job or on his way to something entirely different. An ordinary person becomes extraordinary person or an extraordinary person comes to realize who he really is or finally finds his way. EX: AS GOOD AS IT GETS – Who's the villain? The best villains or opposition characters believe they are doing the right thing; they wouldn't characterize themselves as villains. The opposition character often has difficulty recognizing another person's view of reality or needs.

Details

Details are little things that mean a lot. Idiosyncrasies, habits, quirks, imperfections, and other characterizations will add a lot to a character. They make the character a distinct individual. Personal expressions make a difference. Tiny characterizations (Roger Rabbit's stutter at "Please") ass believability and definition of a character. How does your character handle the little things? If it's right for your character, give them a specialized knowledge or skill, such as computer hacking skills. Props have been used with good effect – weapons (Indy Jones whip), costumes (ball bearings in AS GOOD AS IT GETS). Coincidences should generally work against your character – make it difficult for them to achieve goal. Don't bail her out at end as she should become the most active character in the final act.

A Writer Who Cares

Your central character must have a life and voice of their own. Show you care by researching to really know your characters. Observe them then emerging on the page as real. The best thing is when the characters take over the story and tell you what they want to do. To research, observe people, noting in a small notebook. Search your mind, your own experience, people you've known who can serve as character prototypes, places you've seen, etc. Investigate, explore, and create your character's background: educational background; ethnic, cultural, and religious roots; a professional or work history; past and present social connections and a family of some kind, and a particular way of speaking. Take trips to the library for information, or to a place of business to understand your character's occupation. Interview someone of a particular ethnic group, or even visit a neighborhood. Don't assume you can get by cause you seen movies of same subject matter. Buy someone's lunch to get an interview. Write a character biography or detailed character profile to allow fully drawn characters. Your character's physical description is little importance to the script – focus on physical details essential to the story; a few lines or words that gives us essence of the story, something actors can act. Physiology: What kinds of emotions does your character portray? What is her disposition? How does he handle relationships? Identify complexes, phobias, pet peeves, fears, secrets, attitudes, beliefs, addictions, prejudices, inhibitions, frustrations, habits, superstitions, and moral stands. Is your character extroverted, introverted, aggressive or passive, intuitive or analytical? How does he solve problems? How does she deal with stress? In what way is he screwed up?

Reflect and ask questions:

- What are my character's values?
- What does my character do when she is all alone?
- What's the most traumatic thing ever happened to my character?
- What is the biggest secret?
- What is her most poignant moment?
- What are his hobbies?
- What special abilities does she have?
- What is his deepest fear?
- What kind of underwear does she wear?
- Which end of the toothpaste does he squeeze?
- What is the worst thing that could happen to my character?
- What is the best thing that could happen?

- What is my character doing tonight?

Create aspects to the character that makes her stand apart from all other movie characters. Give your character a contradiction or traits that exist in opposition, such as a clumsy beautiful woman. Identify one or more loveable imperfections as well. Certain things will stand out – select those that say the most about your character and relate the best to your story. Your character will be unique and multi-faced. It doesn't matter when you do the research during the writing process so long as it is done. You could wait till later to fit demands of the script.

Strong Supporting Cast

Add more characters. Emphasize relationships. Some work best because of opposite personalities, the characters are rivals, or similar interests and goals. In your cast, at least one central character, one opposition character, and a confidant (sidekick) whom your central character can talk to. The confidant sometimes performs the additional function of lending contrast to central character. In dramas, they can create necessary comic relief, though this can be done by other characters. You'll probably want a love interest who may function in another role. They may carry the theme or message of the story: ex: mathematician in JURASSIC PARK. Sometimes a shape-shifter adds a twist to the story. Have contrasts in characters and in many levels, from attitudes to methods to social status. Each character must do something to move the story forward.

Good Character

Motivation, Dialogue, Believability. Heart and soul and nervous system of screenplay. Through characters viewers experience emotions.

What is character?

Action is character – what a person does is what he is, not what he says. A good character is made up of background, personality, conflict. Especially dramatic need, point of view, change, and attitude.

- **Dramatic need:** What your character wants to win, gain, get, or achieve during course of story. Must have conflict. Knowing this need holds the elements of character in place.

• **Point of View:** the way the character sees the world. Needs a definite point of view to be good character. Will act, not react, from point of view.

• **Change:** Does your character go through change, if so what is it?

• **Attitude:** Allows you to add dimension to your characters. Positive VS negative, happy VS sad, etc.

Tools of Character

Use anything to help you make a character – 3x5 cards, outline, etc. It must work for you.

• **Character biography:** From birth until time begins in screenplay. Helps you form a character. Name, Age, Birthplace, Relationship with family, early life, what traits are they? Educational level, life in school and threw growing up since birth. As help, write your own biography. Define personal, private, and professional aspects of life, including relationships/interactions with other people.

• **Research:** Interview people for ideas. Interview people who match your character: if plumber, interview a plumber. Find books on subject. At least 3 books. Other kinds of resources outside of three books.

• **Dialogue:** Write lots and rewrite it to get better. It is a function of character. Use tools to help – a tape recorder to record people. People talk in fragments, run-on sentences, incomplete thoughts, changing mood and subject with blink of an eye. Good, effective dialogue will move the story forward and keep the reader turning the pages. It needs to communicate facts and information to the reader or audience. It reveals character. Exposition will expose a character through dialogue, voiceovers on photos, etc. About one scene devoted to exposition – too much is bad. Dialogue establishes relationships between characters and comments on action, connects scenes, ties script together and makes a very effective cinematic tool. You must learn to get to know your characters.

The Visual Dynamics of Character

Film is a visual medium – you tell your story in pictures so we can see the story. Visual action reveals character. Film must convey things about character.

Physical description: briefly describe your character. Do not take any more than 4 sentences, and be specific. Be brief, lucid, and to the point. Ex: In cars, don't specify year, make, model, or color. Setting can also reveal character. Show things about your character. Use the dynamic interaction between picture and sound. Don't say what you show, just show it. Sound track and picture tracks complements the other and broadens your story and character. Voice-over is very effective cinematic device. Still photographs, scrapbooks, photo albums, newspaper headlines, and other mementos can create this kind of visual dynamic.

If you want to write a scene or sequence showing a series of scenes or stills with dialogue voice-over, write the dialogue first without regard to the visuals. Make sure to tighten the dialogue as much as possible. On another page, indicate still pictures or scenes in the order which you want to use them. For stills, describe on a 3x5 card. Don't use more than four or five stills in the sequence. When they are written, take a third sheet and inter cut them. Polish the scene, weaving word and image together, tightly. Smooth out the transitions until the sequence flows.

The flashback inter cuts a scene in the present with a scene from the past. Fragments can fragment a scene, a whole scene, or most of the movie. Flashbacks are generally overused. They need only to expand your story if you are inventive. Film does in present time unless you need to reveal something essential; don't impede the flow of action. Structure flashbacks carefully. Other visual dynamics: character writes in journal or diary, flashforwards, special effects. Let the story and characters tell you what you can and can't use.

◆ ◆ ◆

12

SYNOPSES, OUTLINES & TREATMENTS

These three terms present the novice Screenwriter with a headache, arising from their interchangeability of meaning; one person's Treatment is another's Outline, is yet another's Synopsis.There are many suggested functions and lengths for each form. I will therefore offer my interpretation of the terms; how I define them to navigate my own weary path through the minefield.

Synopses

Synopsis to commit the skeleton of the story to paper, right at the outset – the basic beginning, middle and end written in as close to one page of single-spaced A4 as possible. At this stage, it is little more than an exercise to list the major story events in chronological order. A synopsis is a document I use to help clarify my ideas. When you have worked out the main story events, write a linear synopsis to assist you in holding the full picture in your mind. Remember, as your story evolves, these events will change. Don't spend too much time rewriting the synopsis to reflect these changes because it takes precious time away from the script.When your story has its full complement of incidents write a 'final' synopsis, again keeping as close to a single page as you can.

Outlines

When you are confident you have identified all the major story events, you may find the outline, or step-outline, is a useful tool to co-develop story and plot.This is a method of outlining the bare bones of each scene on 5"×3" or 6"×4" lined index cards. The bare bones consist of: the slug line, characters present and a brief description of the action.The general rule is, if you can't fit the description on one side of the card, the scene may be too long and you should consider breaking it down. It's a good idea to write in pencil, as your scenes will evolve. Number your cards, again in pencil.The average length of a feature film scene is around two minutes, so 50-60 scenes/cards give you the skeleton of a feature script (remember, a scene change occurs whenever there is a change of location and/or time). Don't worry too much if you have lots of short scenes totalling more than 60 cards.

This can be a good thing, especially in fast-paced action scripts;American films average nearly twice as many scenes as British or European films. Find a large wall or floor space where you can experiment with the order of your scenes to develop your plot – even if you think it will run chronologically, you may want to play around with sub-plots. Like the synopsis, the step-outline is for the writer's benefit and offers a user-friendly way to juggle events and arrive at the best dramatic framework for the plot.

Treatments

A treatment is usually written either when the story events are almost complete and require a more expanded and detailed document than a synopsis, or when the final draft script is ready for marketing. Writing an early treatment is advisable; it helps you to work out plot problems before attempting your first draft.

Although a treatment is excellent for getting a grip on the complexity of the plot and clarifying your thoughts, it is primarily a selling document to market yourself and your product. Increasingly, producers and agents are asking to read treatments.They can tell from the treatment whether or not the script (and the writer) will interest them, and it takes less time to read. The upside for the writer is that very good treatments open a lot of important doors; the downside is they may later discover they're better at writing treatments than they are at writing scripts and their beloved project may be passed to someone else.

Treatments should be regarded as an addition to a script, never as a replacement. Ultimately, no matter how good your treatment, the quality of your script remains the most important criterion on which you will be judged.

The treatment comprehensively documents the major incidents of the plot. It is written in the present tense, single-spaced, and contains the five Ws and an H: who, what, where, when, why and how;including (importantly) the end.The style should be pared down, flowing and entertaining to the reader. Broad strokes, no confusion or ambiguity, conveying the emotional impact of the story. There is little consensus on an ideal length, anything over five pages is generally accepted as a treatment. Thirty- or even sixty-page treatments are not unheard of, but such detail is unnecessary and defeats the object of providing agents and producers with a short selling document.The time would be better spent developing your script.

◆ ◆ ◆

13

PRINCIPLES OF SCENE WRITING

1. You must create a movie in the mind of the reader.

2. Nothing goes on the page that doesn't go on the screen.

3. There are three uses for any screenplay: as a proposal; as a blueprint (shooting script); and as a record, for postproduction.

4. There must be nothing in the screenplay which you know you can improve.

5. Improper format reduces the reader's emotional involvement.

Screenplays are always written in present tense.

Writing Descriptions

Write character and setting description that is concise, clever, provocative, and detailed and that conveys the essence of a character or setting, rather than mere physical description, which might limit casting. Two or three word phrases for character and setting best. Ex: "an aging, dusty Underwood" NOT "typewriter"; for characters, describe clothing, hair style, movement, surroundings, habits, or physical details (scars, deformities, or expressions, attitudes, limited reference to background. Ex: (from Body Heat) TEDDY LAURSEN, rock and roll arsonist... Another ex: Earl's every movement projects the ten years he's spent pumping iron (limited background reference).Only go into detail if necessary for plot. Never mention actor names!

Writing Action

In writing action, your primary goal is clarity. Use everyday, straightforward language (a high school reading level). Stay away from convoluted words and phrases, excessive technical jargon, and impressive but tedious vocabulary. Lengthen the action and description passages, not the dialogue or unnecessary scenes. Use action words. Instead of "go", use walk, run, crawl, fly leap, hurtle, dart, or shuffle down the street. Give your action scenes to someone to read. If the reader confuses something, change it to make it better.

Do NOT write: They jump into their cars and there is a terrific chase.

Instead:

As the black limousine comes racing toward Jimmie, he leaps onto the sideboard of a passing ice cream wagon. Opening the door of the moving truck, he pushes the startled driver off the seat and guns the accelerator.

The limousine fishtails toward Jimmie and the truck, sideswiping a light pole and narrowly missing a young girl on her tricycle.

Soon the limo is bearing down on Jimmie's truck at close to 90 miles an hour as he thunders toward an irrigation ditch...

Dialogue

Ask the following questions about any scene before writing dialogue:

- What is my objective?
- How will the scene end?
- What is each character's objective?
- What is each character's attitude?
- How will the scene begin?

The Rewrite

Writing a screenplay is a process. Many people writing their first screenplay believe that all they have to do is write it, then have it typed up and sent out. Nothing is further from the truth. Writing is a day-by-day job, three to five hours a day, five days a week, typing pages over and over again, cutting strips of paper and pasting them on the master pages. Rewriting your screen- play is necessary; it corrects the changes you've made during the first words-on-paper draft, then clarifies and defines your story and sharpens your characters and situations.

Writing a first-draft screenplay is done in three stages; first, the words-on-paper draft, which you've just finished; second, the "mechanical" stage, where you correct changes made during the writing, and third, the "polish" stage.

When you complete the first words-on-paper draft, you're ready to begin the second stage, the "mechanical" stage; you'll correct the changes you made during the first stage, bring the script to length, tighten up the dramatic tension, and sharpen the focus of your main character. In this stage of the screenwriting process you're going to be changing things, a lot of things; you'll rewrite 80 percent of Act I, about 60 percent of the first half of Act II, about 25 percent of the second half of Act II, and about 10 or 15 percent of Act III. Then you'll go into the third stage of the first draft, polishing, accenting, texturing each scene, changing a word here, a word there, a sentence here, a scene there, some- times rewriting a scene some 10 or 15 times to make it right. After you finish the first words-on-paper draft, and take a week to 10 days off, it's time to get back to work and begin the second stage of your screenplay. This rewrite of the first words-onpaper draft is the "mechanical" draft.

That's just what it is. Don't expect creative inspiration to guide you, because you're going to be correcting all those changes you made in the first and second act so your story line progresses from beginning to end. You've got to set it up properly, add new scenes that make it work, and delete those scenes that don't. You're going to be typing a lot in this draft, so be prepared for it. The first thing you have to do is see what you've got. You probably don't know or remember what you did in the first act; when you're in the paradigm, you can't see the paradigm. You have no overview, no objective perspective about what you've done or not done. The first thing you have to do is get an overview. The way to do that is read the entire first draft in one sitting from beginning to end. Do not take notes or write in the margins about the changes you want to make.

You might experience several emotional swings: "This is the worst thing I've ever read," is the most common response. "It's just awful, terrible." Your attitude should be simple: you know your script needs work, so you don't need anyone to tell you what you already know. How good or bad it is at this stage is absolutely irrelevant. What happens most of the time is that you get on a roller coaster; you'll like some of it, you'll hate some of it.

A rewrite is essential to make what you've written better. Accept it, don't argue with it, and don't fight it. That's just the way it is. Nobody ever told you writing a screenplay was going to be a piece of cake.

When you complete reading the words-on-paper draft, think about it. Make mental notes, nothing else. Notice what you have to do to set up those changes you made during Act II, and any other things you need to do to make the script work. Think about it a few hours, or better yet, let it cook overnight. You don't need to make any clearcut or defined decisions at this point. You'll be working in 30-page units of action. You'll rewrite Act I, then the first half of Act II, then the second half of Act II, and then Act III. You'll do most of the work in Act I. You're going to rewrite about 80 percent of this material.

Now read Act I and make extensive notes, either on the margin or on a pad. Any dialogue changes, scene changes, or shifts in action, plot, or character, will need to be integrated into the script as a whole. When you know the changes you want to make, do new scene cards for Act I. Some scenes will be okay the way they are; some will not. Just take your 3 x 5 cards and lay them out for the new Act I.

You'll probably need to write about five or six new scenes, change some of the dialogue in several scenes, and then polish, trim, and cut to length. This process should take about two weeks. Usually, Act I takes the longest time of the rewrite. Rewriting the first act will be easier than you thought it would be. You've already established your writing discipline, and you know your story, so the execution of these changes should be easy and natural. Sometimes you might have difficulty deciding what to do, especially if Act I is too long. If that happens, you might need to transfer a few scenes from Act I to Act II. Just do the rewrite for Act I. Work in to-page units, and strive for clarity and simplicity of visual image. Tell your story, one scene at a time, one page at a time. Concentrate on opening up your story visually. You'll find in Act I you had a tendency to tell most of your story with dialogue. You'll "talk" your story. For example, your character may be driving a car and see a jewelry store.

"I need a jade ring," your character says to her mother. "Let's stop." You end the scene and then cut to the next scene, where she shows off her new jade ring at a party. This time show it; go inside the store, show your character standing at the counter buying the ring, then cut to the party scene. Show your character walking in the park, jogging on the streets. Think visually; be aware of cinematic transitions, how you go from one scene into another; watch your lead ins and lead outs. When you finish Act I, go back and clean it up a bit. Polish a scene or retype some pages, cut out a few lines of dialogue to make it clearer and tighter. Don't spend too much time on it; it's important to move forward through the screenplay; always work from beginning to end, beginning to end.

Move on to the first half of Act II. Read it and take notes on what you need to do to make it work. You'll find you'll be changing about 60 percent of the first half. Determine the changes you want to make, then layout this section on 3 X 5 cards, just like Act I. Know your dramatic context; make sure Pinch I is clean and tight and the midpoint clear and defined. If you need to do anything to make your story work, do it. Tell your story visually. Try to cut down your dialogue scenes by focusing on the visual dynamics. Let Pinch I keep your story on track.

Does the midpoint still work effectively? Is it too long or too short? Do you need to redefine it visually? Write the midpoint. You'll spend a week or two on this section. Move on to the second half of Act II. Read it through. Make notes on what you need to do to correct the changes. Structure the second half on fourteen 3 x 5 cards. Once you know what you need to do, execute it simply, keeping the dramatic context and time frame clearly in mind. You probably won't have to change more than 25-30 percent of the second half of Act II. Keep your story on track. Follow your main character through the development of your story; move forward through Pinch II and Plot Point II. When you finished, don't spend too much time polishing this section because you'll spend a lot of time in doubt and confusion, and the creative urge might disappear. This section will only take you about a week to correct.

In Act III, you'll only need to rewrite about 10-15 percent of the words-on-paper draft. This will take you about a week. You might want to clean up and define your ending, refocus the resolution. The actual writing process itself at this time is clear-cut and simple to handle; you know exactly what you have to do to finish it. If you have a large action sequence for your ending- like the destruction of the new Death Star in Return of the Jedi-you may want to draw a picture or "storyboard" what will happen.

A screenplay is a story told in pictures, dialogue, and description. It didn't matter that I was making up a location; if the film was made, the script would be changed to fit the actual location site. Don't worry about whether the "exact" location exists; simply be clear about what you want to write, then write it. You should be able to finish this "mechanical" draft of your screenplay in about four to five weeks, and it should end up being anywhere from 110 to 120 pages, no longer. Your story line should be clear, with all the necessary changes fused into an organic story line from beginning to end. You may or may not want to take a few days or a week off. Do what you want. You're ready to move into the third, or polish, stage of your first-draft screenplay.

This is where you'll really write your screenplay. You'll be typing a lot. The process of rewriting entails more typing than writing. You'll move three lines from a scene in Act I to another scene in the first half of Act II. You may type it up on a strip of paper and paste it on the page. You'll bridge one scene with another scene, and drop the transition; you'll telescope scenes; that is, you may take a scene from Act I, combine it with a scene in Act II, and end up with a scene shorter than either. You'll accent, polish, hone, tighten, and texture your script; it's the most important stage of the screenwriting experience. You'll notice rhythm of action, you'll see places where a "pause," or a "beat" will strengthen the suspense of your scene. You'll reword; "he looks at the woman across from him," may become "he regards her questioningly." You'll sharpen visual images by adding adjectives, tighten and condense dialogue by cutting words from speeches, sometimes whole sentences, occasionally chunks of dialogue.

Again, work in 30-page units of action; do Act I, then the first half of Act II, then the second half of Act II, then Act III. Working in units like this allows you to control your story and move forward, step by step, toward the resolution.

Good structure, remember, is the relationship between the parts and the whole; it is like an ice cube and water, or fire and its heat. As you're polishing your screenplay, you'll subdue the structural elements until they are integral to the story.

Polish Act I. Read it, typing and cleaning it up as you move through scenes and pages. Cross out a sentence here, add a few words there, bridge this paragraph with this line of dialogue, and so on. Tighten, trim, condense, polish, cut, cut, and cut some more. Most new writers don't like to cut words-or paragraphs-but you've got to be ruthless in this stage. If you're wondering whether you should keep this dialogue, paragraph, description, or scene, chances are you'll need to cut it.

The purpose of the polish stage is to make it the best screenplay you can. How do you know when the rewrite's done? When can you lay down your pages and say "I've completed the first draft of my screenplay"? It's a difficult question. You never really know, but there are certain signs to look for. First of all, understand that your script will never be perfect. There will always be a few scenes that don't work. No matter how many times you write and rewrite, they'll never be right. You'll have to let those scenes go.

The Good Read

The writer's job is to keep the reader turning pages. What does the reader look for?

Story, character, and style, first and foremost. The first thing that attracts me is the writing style, the way the words are put down on paper: lean, tight, crisp, and visual. Then the premise. Does it grab my attention? Is it interesting? How is the script set up in terms of story, and visual dynamics? Are the characters well-rounded and threedimensional? Is there enough information presented during the first ten pages to make me want to continue reading? When you find a "good read," you know it; there's a certain excitement and energy on the first page.

People hate to read in Hollywood, yet everybody loves to read a good screenplay. Things never change in that respect.

A reader's evaluation sheet from a major film company:

GENRE:

Brief SYNOPSIS: a four- or five-line description of what the story is about; the subject of the screenplay.

Detailed Summary: one-and-a-half page detailed summary of the story, in depth and detail

I - Character

A) Design:

B) Development:

II-Dialogue

III. Structure

A) Design:

B) Development:

C) Pacing:

D) Resolution:

Reader's recommendation:

What's the reader going to say about your screenplay? As an exercise you might want to familiarize yourself with this evaluation. This is where the reader comes from. From his or her point of view there's always another script to read; usually the pile on the desk is about two feet high. Everybody's writing screenplays, and when the readers read the scripts, 99 times out of 100 they are disappointed.

Each Rewrite

With each successive rewrite, polish the dialogue so that it:

• Contributes to the scene's objective and the overall outer motivation for your hero

• Is consistent with the characters

• Reveals character background, inner motivation or conflict, or theme, when appropriate

• Is as clever, funny, original, provocative, interesting, and enjoyable to read as is appropriate

Second and Third Draft Completed

When the second or third draft is completed, apply the following checklist:

• How does the scene contribute to the hero's outer motivation?

• Does the scene possess a beginning, middle, and an end?

• Does the scene thrust the reader into the following scenes?

• What is each character's objective?

• What is each character's attitude?

• Does the scene contain action, not just dialogue?

• Does the scene serve multiple functions? A single scene can employ:

character background, inner motivation, inner conflict and identification, theme, humor, exposition, and structural devices (superior positioning, foreshadowing, echoing, etc.). Some scenes should contain nothing but action.

Do the needs of other primaries:

1. Are your Romance, Nemesis, and Reflection defined in terms of the Hero's outer motivation when they are introduced?

2. Are all of your primary characters introduced by the beginning of Act 2?

3. Once a primary character is introduced, are there any long gaps on the chart where the character doesn't appear? This is a danger signal. A primary character must appear regularly throughout the screenplay unless the character dies. Otherwise, the character is not fulfilling her necessary function.

4. Is there an "arc" to each primary character's story? In other words, do your Nemesis, Reflection, and Romance all possess clear outer motivations, and are those desires built up and resolved by the end of the screenplay?

5. Do the primary characters other than the hero interact? This won't always occur, but as a general rule, your screenplay will be stronger if your reflection, nemesis, and/or romance confront each other. Such scenes will provide opportunities for added conflict, humor, and character revelation and will help prevent a monotonous story line involving only your hero.

6. Does each of your primary characters have at least one "big moment"? It's nice if you can create a particularly dramatic, funny, or revealing scene or two for characters besides your hero. As with the previous item on this list, such moments will add depth, texture, and emotional involvement to your screenplay.

Such scenes can also help commercially, when it's time to

cast the movie.

About Formats

There is no such thing as **THE** correct format. That's why every book on formatting has slightly different formatting rules.

BUT (a big but), there is **proper** format.

What does this mean? Simply, that there's not just **one** way to format scripts, but a range of ways that are acceptable. Some books say that a film script's left margin should be 1.5". Others say that it should be 1.7" Both of those are right. Nobody's going to look at your script, pull out a ruler and scream, "One point six-four inches! You'll never work in this town again!" But a 1" left margin... that's not right. That's out of the acceptable range and could piss off a producer who thinks you're trying to trick him into thinking your script is shorter than it really is.

Why is there a range and not a single way? Who knows. Individual preference, often. Changing tastes over time, usually. But sometimes it's a more obnoxious reason. Some TV shows have a unique format just so they can tell if a writer submitting to that show has done her homework.

If the writer's script is not in that unique format, the producers can say to themselves, "Well, we're obviously not important enough for the writer to have checked to see how **WE** do it! No thank you." It's petty, but it's true. Don't worry, though, we'll tell you how to avoid that situation.

Like most rules, the ones in here are meant to be used whenever possible, but broken when necessary. None of this is etched in stone, but you can't go wrong by following it religiously. If you have a really good reason for doing it differently; if that rule-breaking formatting choice tells your story better than anything we describe... go for it. Just don't be cavalier and think that you're story is unique and, therefore NEEDS unique formatting. Remember, the odds are that the greatest scripts you can think of were written using these rules, not some weird, random ones.

From the formatting and style standpoint, a script is nothing but a collection of elements. From the element standpoint, the key to successful formatting and powerful writing is knowing what the elements are, how and when to use them and how they should look.

Presentation – Things to Do AFTER You're Done

If a producer or such request a certain format, use it! Check with screenplays written by the studio to write yours that way.

List of No-Nos:

- No fancy covers, artwork, illustrations, storyboards.
- Don't number the scenes.
- No justified right margins.
- Don't write CONTINUED at the top and bottom of each page.
- Don't bold or italicize.
- Avoid camera and editing directions
- Don't use a dot-matrix printer. Photocopies are okay.
- Don't date your script.
- Don't mention a draft.
- No suggested cast list or character bios unless requested.
- No list of characters or sets.
- Don't include a synopsis unless requested.
- Don't include a budget.
- No headers or footers except page numbers.

Page Breaks

The first script line on every page should be 1" from the top of the page. The Header, if any, is 1/2" from the top.

Never end a page with a Scene Heading... unless another Scene Heading is the first thing at the top of the next page.

Never end a page with a Shot... unless another Shot is the

first thing at the top of the next page.

Never start a page with a Transition.

If you need to put a page break in the middle of some Action, you can only break the page after at least 2 lines of Action, and only at the end of a sentence. Some studios also insist that the Action at the top of the next page have at least 2 lines as well. If you can't split the Action to fit this rule, don't split it and move the entire Action onto the next page (some people will argue that you don't need to split Action — just move it to the next page. Why would you do this when it might unnecessarily add pages to your script?).

Never put a page break between a Scene Heading and a Cast List (in TV and Sitcom scripts).

Never put a page break after a Cast List element.

Never put a page break before an END OF ACT or END OF SCENE indicator.

Never put a page break after a Character Name.

If you have a Parenthetical directly under a Character name, never put a page break after that Parenthetical.

If you need a page break in the middle of Dialogue, you can only break the page after at least 2 lines of Dialogue, and only at the end of the sentence. If you have a Parenthetical in the middle of some Dialogue,

like this:

HILLARY

I really wanted to be President myself,

but I knew that there was no way...

(beat)

Unless... well, I couldn't do that, now

could I?

... you cannot put a page break after the Parenthetical, but you have the option of putting one before it if you need to (in other words, it's a valid place to put a page break, but it's your own stylistic choice as to whether you do — we do). Regardless, when you split

Dialogue with a page break, put the word "more" or "MORE" in parenthesis on the line after the Dialogue in the same margins as the Character Name. Then, at the top of the next page, repeat the Character

Name before the Dialogue and add the Extension (CONT'D) or (cont'd). It's a personal preference for whether you use the uppercase or lowercase "cont'd" and "more."

◆ ◆ ◆

14

Need for Storytelling

We need look no further than the number of television channels—to say nothing of the number of hours that television broadcasts news stories, sports stories, nonfiction stories, and fiction stories, stories of all lengths—to realize the number of stories available to the public every day. Add the number of films, newspapers and magazines, and oral stories (from jokes to anecdotes to elaborate tales, from gossip to reportage, from free association to analytic interpretation), and it is evident we are all telling stories. There are stories on every level, from casual to the most meaningful.

It's not so much that we hunger for any one kind of story but rather that we need a full range of stories. Human experience functions on a wide band, from superficial to deeply meaningful, and storytelling reflects that human experience.

Why do we need stories? We need them to help us make sense of our world, both the past and the present so we can make our way to a future.

But there are other reasons stories have been important, beyond the need to understand, and one is the need of the teller to communicate. Whether in pantomime or Elizabethan tragedy, storytellers want to communicate with others.

The cave painter and the short-film director may have different means, but both want to use their medium to bind artist and audience together for that instant or that half-hour of the storytelling experience. For that time, storyteller and audience become a community, with all the historical implications of the relationship between artist and audience.

Another reason for storytelling is the education of the community. Many cultures have used storytelling to educate, particularly about the ethics of living in the society. The passing on of tradition and ethics has been a central focus of storytelling, from the fairy tale to the fable to the documentary film. Finally, storytelling provides a legitimate access route to the world of our dreams and our fears; it provides an outlet for both of these types of psychic experiences.

The goal of the story is to incorporate these dimensions of life into consciousness. Dreams and fears are important elements of storytelling.

STORYTELLING STRATEGIES

Although screen stories have unique qualities particular to film, screen stories for both short and long films often share characteristics with other kinds of storytelling. In this chapter, we will discuss those general qualities and suggest links to other forms of storytelling, forms that provide the first and best source of material for short films.

STORY QUALITIES

All stories must engage the curiosity of an audience, whether that audience be one or a thousand. The storyteller must build on that curiosity, inviting our involvement in a character's situation, and finally allow the viewer to identify with the character and the situation.

To hold the audience and move it through the story, a variety of devices are used. Some are operating principles; others are artificial techniques. But no matter what device is used, the goal is the same—to move the audience from curiosity to a more emotional state. If the story works, the results can range from amusement to tragedy. In each case, it is the storytelling qualities that transcend the medium and hold the audience's attention.

These story qualities can be broken down into two groups: *character qualities*, and *plot qualities*. The primary character quality of a story is that we have to identify with the main character if we are to be engaged with the story. We have to become concerned with his or her dilemma, and we have to care about the outcome.

In order to identify with the characters, we have to know who they are and how they've arrived at the point where we join the story. A main character may be active or passive, young or old, male or female.

These qualities should be specific and appropriate to the story; it is no use telling a story about a passive Olympic athlete, because the drive to become an Olympic athlete requires, by definition, a forceful rather than passive character. Specificity about culture, family, and career is also helpful in creating a person we recognize.

What are the person's goals? What are his or her hopes, dreams, fears? Any or all of these details can also help create a recognizable character. That recognition is the first step toward identification—if we recognize the character and his or her situation, we will begin to connect with the character.

As much as our identification with the main character relies on our recognizing and caring about the character, that identification can be equally influenced by the role of the antagonist. The antagonist can be a mountain, a desert, or a raging storm; it can be an angry father, an overprotective mother, or an unjust boss. Often the most interesting antagonist of all can be one's self: our own flaws (fear, greed, anger, passivity) can play the role of the enemy.

As we have observed, the more forceful the antagonist in a story, the greater the struggle of the protagonist. If the goal of the story is to portray heroic behavior, the role of the antagonist can be crucial. If the goal is more to portray realism and complexity in the protagonist's actions, here too the character of the antagonist is critical.

It is notable that the characters of the protagonist and antagonist are frequently opposites, often in appearance as well as behavior. This *polarity* of protagonist and antagonist is the most overt use of opposites in storytelling. Polarized characteristics are also used with characters other than protagonists or antagonists, and to good effect. The greater the number of polarities in the story, the greater the conflict and the resulting interest to the reader, listener, or viewer. Polarity is an extremely useful storytelling device.

Plot qualities are closely related to character, but because they involve events outside of character, they can be considered separately. Agood example of this notion is the role of conflict in storytelling: the more powerful the barriers that stand in the way of the character achieving his or her goal, the more compelling the plot. If the character faces no barriers in achieving his or her goal, there is no story.

This is the nature and the role of conflict in storytelling— to provide barriers to the characters and their goals.

What if the character does not have a goal? This will pose a problem for developing a conflict. What if the character's goal is unrealistic? The storyteller may focus on the conflict inherent in discovering that the goal is unattainable. In both examples, the linkage of conflict to character is intentional.

Plot cannot stand alone, outside of character, without the story suffering because of it. Character, plot, and conflict are intricately related to one another. One dimension of conflict is how much a character wants to achieve his or her goal. Does the character want, desire, or need to achieve this goal? The greater the desire of the character, the greater the potential for conflict. The parallel with regard to the plot is also true: the more powerful the resistance, whether through the antagonist or other forces, the greater the conflict potential.

Remember that barriers to the character's goal may be external (a place, another person) or internal. What is most important to the story is that the viewers or readers understand that the barriers are the source of conflict for the character. From the most simple fable, such as "The Tortoise and the Hare," to a complex short story, such as Hemingway's "The Snows of Kilimanjaro," the sources of conflict are clear to the readers, and as the story progresses they become clear to the protagonist.

Whether the character succeeds in the conflict, as in "The Tortoise and the Hare," or fails, as in "The Snows of Kilimanjaro," it is the struggle to overcome the barriers that is the fabric of the story. In each case, the motivation of the protagonist to triumph over conflict seems primal, and that desire fuels our identification and understanding.

Good stories tend to have a powerful conflict associated with a character we understand and whose desire fuels the story.

The first notable characteristic of a good story is that it presents an interesting interpretation of a situation that, on one level, we have seen before.

Aspecific example will illustrate this. We are all familiar with the experience of the first day of school; the situation conjures up all kinds of associations for each person. Building on our familiarity with this situation, we can make it more interesting and arouse curiosity by introducing a new factor—the age of the new student.

What if the new student in the local high school is 40 years old, and he is joining a class full of 14-year-olds? The key here is that there is comfort for the viewer or reader in known situations—birthdays, weddings, funerals, and first days of school. The good storyteller uses our knowledge of the situation and whets our appetite for the story by introducing a new element.

Another factor in the plot is that point at which the storyteller chooses to join the story. It is crucial that the writer joins the story at a point where the dramatic possibilities can be maximized. The goal of the storyteller is to energize the tale, and the point of entry is critical in accomplishing this goal.

For example, we join Ambrose Bierce's short story "An Occurrence at Owl Creek Bridge" at the point when a civilian has been caught trespassing on a bridge held by Union soldiers during the Civil War. Will the unfortunate Southerner die for his transgression, or escape to safety? This question forms the substance of the story that unfolds.

At the beginning of Raymond Carver's short story "Cathedral," a blind man, who has recently lost his wife, plans to visit an old friend and her husband. The issue is whether the friend's rocky marriage can bear a visitation from a sightless rival. The main character is the husband in the problematic relationship. The announcement of the visit is the point at which we join the story.

Good storytellers will find a point to join a story that will serve to generate tension and attract attention. If we do not join the story at such a point, not only is dramatic opportunity lost, but the chance to harness the audience's curiosity will be lost, too. We will, in effect, be waiting for the story to begin.

To summarize, an interesting situation, a strong entry point, and enough conflict are necessary to start the story.

PLOT STRATEGIES

In order to carry us through the story, the storyteller relies on two plot strategies— *surprise* (or *reversal*), and a *rising level of action* in the course of the plot. Surprise is critical, because if we are maintained on a steady diet of what we expect, we become bored and leave the story.

Part of the storyteller's task is to keep us from getting bored: to maintain, use, and stimulate our curiosity about the story.

Surprise may be found in an unexpected plot twist or an unexpected behavior on the part of the character. In either case, the reversal or surprise upsets our expectations; it maintains and builds upon our curiosity.

Think about your favorite film or fairy tale. How often in the course of the film or the fairy tale are you surprised by the course of events? Just as we both suffer through and enjoy a roller coaster ride, we enjoy a similar pattern of plot movement in a script.

A notable difference between the roller coaster ride and a

story, however, is that in the scenes, there tends to be a pattern of *rising action* rather than the peaks and valleys of a carnival ride. That rising action means that the surprises in the plot become more intense as we move through the story.

Only through this progression of greater surprises can the story move toward a climax.

Just as every joke has a punch line, every story has a climax. The climax is the payoff, the point at which the character's efforts against all odds are successful (or unsuccessful, in some cases).

The climax is the high point of the script, and for many storytellers the very reason for their writing, telling, or filming it. Without a rising level of action, this culmination would not be a climax but merely another event in the story. Consequently, the action in the climactic scene tends to have an all-or-nothing quality. It is the scene in which the stakes are highest for the main character.

Every good short script also has a sense of resolution. Too often the climax is mistaken for the resolution; the resolution is the *aftermath* of the climax. The resolution brings us back to an even state after having experienced a growing feeling of intensity. The resolution in terms of the plot is the very end of the plot.

REALISM VERSUS FANTASY

A general decision made by every storyteller, one that will affect how powerfully the audience engages the story, is the choice of *realism* or *fantasy* as the storytelling mode. Good stories can be realistic or fantastic, but the choice will affect how the storyteller utilizes character and plot, among other things. If a story is realistic, the detailing of the plot and of character has to be convincing and recognizable.

If, on the other hand, the choice is fantasy, the characterizations will be more representational or metaphorical. Realistic characterization is complex, believable, recognizable; in a fantasy, characters may represent a class, gender, or race. In other words, a character may be used as a metaphor for a purpose that serves the story, in this case a fantasy. Consequently, the level of detail will tend to be less.

Plot, on the other hand, will become that much more important, because the character in a fantasy is not as easy to identify with as a realistic character would be. Therefore, the plot needs to involve the viewer more actively than the character alone can.

The choice between realism and fantasy will help the storyteller determine how to employ the other storytelling elements; devices such as surprises and twists and turns of plot are even more important in fantasy. The narrative devices are the writer's tools. In choosing a realist approach, the author opts for character devices; in fantasy, he or she opts for plot-oriented devices. Realistic story forms, such as melodrama, rely on identification with the character.

They succeed or fail depending on the effectiveness of that identification. Fantasy is usually effective around a "moral" or a fantastic journey. In fantasy, plot is more crucial than identification with the character.

SOURCES FOR STORYTELLING

Whether your goal is a contemporary story, a story specific to a culture, or a more universal story, there are many sources of inspiration, information, or insight for you to draw from.

Many writers and teachers of writing believe that the best source is your own experience. Our feeling is that your experience is only one of many sources. Should you choose your own experience for a story, the detailing of the story is clearly less problematic.

The problem writers face with their own experience is their loyalty to the memory of that experience—simply retelling something as it happened to you is not storytelling. The personal intensity the writer felt must be shaped using storytelling devices to make the memory more dramatically viable.

Writers can be more personal than Updike (like Clark Blaise), or they can be less personal, as Frederick Forsythe tends to be. Our advice is that personal experience is an excellent source of material, but that considerations of narrative and audience should mediate between the totally subjective and objectified. The goal should always be to create an accessible, engaging story. The personal can often be self-indulgent or sophomoric, whereas a story, based on personal experience, that tries to engage the audience more fully, leaves the audience as witnesses instead of participants.

There are many other sources of stories beyond personal recollection, the most obvious being the daily newspapers. In this chapter, we will illustrate other sources that can be used as the basis for excellent film or video stories.

The Periodical Article as a Source

In February 1992, two years after reunification, the following story was reported from the former East Germany.3 The recently opened Stasi (secret police) files had revealed that a 30-year-old woman who had been involved in a human rights demonstration in the mid-1980s had for the next six years been under observation—and that the spy who had reported her activities throughout this time was her husband. She filed for divorce.

Her husband stated in an interview that if the Communists had remained in control, he would have continued to spy on her.

Here is a marital relationship, which, in an ideal world, we might expect to function to protect husband and wife from the problems and challenges of society—in this case a Communist regime in East Germany.

This expectation proves to be wrong, since the husband represented the intrusive government and spied on his wife, whose activities defied the government's philosophy and policy. What we might expect to be the most cherished haven from Communism and government, the family unit, was therefore no protection for the individual. The implication is that there *is* no protection for the individual.

Although there is sufficient story potential here for a longer film, there are also a number of ways the story can be developed for a short one. The following is one suggestion for a short film script.

There are many points where it would be effective to join this story. We suggest that the drama is least interesting after the public discovery of the husband as a spy. What remains at that point is only resolution—what will happen to the marriage and to the wife and the husband (does he get his comeuppance?). We suggest that the presence of the state is important but needn't be elaborated. We also suggest that the story concentrate on the two characters in the marriage.

A critical choice will be which character should be the main character. If it is to be the wife, the script should focus on the danger of her activities and her expectation that the haven from the danger is her marriage. In this version, she needn't find out that he is a spy, but we in the audience will gradually discover it and realize that she will suffer, without understanding why, for her activities.

On the other hand, if the husband is the main character, we want the story to focus on why a man has to betray his family for the state. Here he may be his own antagonist. The story line should focus not only on his betrayal but also on an understanding of his character.

We should confine the story to a very simple situation—let us say, the day of a human rights march. Let's assume that the woman is our main character. We needn't see the march itself but can confine the film to the preparations for the march and the aftermath. The scenes should clarify the relationship by highlighting the sense of trust on the part of the wife, and the planning and preparation of a report on the part of the husband. The government- controlled media—state radio, television, and newspapers— should be omnipresent. It may be necessary to embody the state in another character—a neighbor, for example.

If the person who represents the state is too far from home—at work, for example—we would dilute the sense of an immediate threat of spies at and near home. The closer the spies, the more intense the story will be.

We can distract the audience from the true nature of the neighbor by making the neighbor an attractive woman. The initial impression should be that the husband is having an affair, rather than reporting to another spy. This way, when we do discover that they are both spies, the surprise and shock will be that much greater. In this political climate, spying, not sex, is practiced by the husband and neighbor as the highest form of leisure and pleasure!

It would be useful if the wife suspects the husband of an affair and if the climax of the film involves her accusation and his admission of an affair with the neighbor. But we in the audience will know that the truth is more sinister. She accepts the affair, and the marriage—and the spying—go on. The story can only grow more suspenseful because of her husband's activities.

This short film will have much in the way of conflict between wife and husband/neighbor/state, but the situation will be simple, no more than "a day in the life" of the characters. When the wife chooses to accept her husband's story of infidelity, we begin to understand that the real danger to the individual is not infidelity but rather the state. Her choice implies much about priorities and life in 1985 East Germany. The approach we have taken in developing a magazine article into a shortfilm outline can be applied to any other source. We move now to a simpler source, the joke.

The Joke

Jokes or anecdotes can readily be the source of a short film, since they have a character, a narrative, and a climax. The writer need only add another character or two and provide a resolution, so that the audience will not be left in an unresolved state regarding the fate of the main character. The following joke will provide a constructive example.

Mark Twain tells the story of trying to get rid of the wreck of an old umbrella. First, he threw it in the ash can, but someone recognized it as his and returned it. Then he dropped it down a deep well, but someone repairing the well saw the umbrella and returned it. He tried several other methods, but always the umbrella came back. "Finally," says Mark Twain, "I lent it to a friend, and I never saw it again."

Not only does this particular joke have a simple narrative, a conflict, and a main character, but it also has interesting opportunities for sound—not dialogue, but rather the use of creative sound effects and music. Indeed, it is possible to envision this script entirely without dialogue. It also has the virtues of visual action and of personal interaction that can be easily understood visually. A short script version should include some action that illustrates why the character needed the umbrella in the first place.

We recommend a time frame of a few hours, beginning with the character preparing to leave the house. His wife reminds him to take the umbrella, because rain is forecast. The character is already resentful. Of course his wife is right, but he doesn't like to be wrong.

He leaves home with a specific errand—to purchase particular foods for dinner. His wife has provided him with a list. He proceeds to the food store but is caught in a terrible downpour. A gust of wind ruins his umbrella just before he reaches the food store. He carries in the ruined umbrella and proceeds to shop. When he's finished, the clouds haven't quite blown over, so he keeps the umbrella. After he has walked about a block, the sun bursts out, and he makes his first attempt to discard the umbrella.

What follows are his three attempts to get rid of the umbrella. Twice he leaves the umbrella in an ash can, and twice a good citizen runs after him with it, first an adult and then a young boy.

Carrying the groceries and now the broken umbrella, he continues on. He drops the umbrella down a well near his home and goes home thinking no more of it. No sooner has he unpacked the groceries than a workman who had been in the well knocks on his door and returns the umbrella. Now he is more than irked. He wants to destroy this ruined umbrella. He can't put it in the garbage; the garbage man will no doubt return the precious object. He can't share the problem with his wife; she will not understand. Then it comes to him. He puts the umbrella back in the closet.

The next day it is raining heavily. He takes the broken

umbrella and a functional one and goes out for a walk in the rain. He sees his friend Don, who is getting wet rushing to the grocery store, list in hand. Our main character displays the spare umbrella under his arm, basking in his dryness from the working umbrella. Naturally, Don asks if he can borrow an umbrella from him. The main character agrees and saunters back home. Don struggles with the broken umbrella. A subtitle tells us that the main character never sees the broken umbrella again.

The Idiom

An idiom can provide an excellent starting point for a short story, since the idiom provides a character as well as an editorial position on that character. It also implies a narrative.

For our example, let's use the idiom "fall guy." According to a slang dictionary, the etymology of "fall guy" is as follows: "By one account, the original fall guy was a wrestler who deliberately 'took a fall'—as commercial ('exhibition') wrestlers are still doing. Well, maybe. In British criminal slang 'fall' has meant 'be arrested' since the 1880s (it derives from a much earlier figurative sense, a descent from moral elevation, as in Adam's fall)." A fall guy, then, is someone paid or framed to "fall" for a crime; as Sam Spade explains it to the Fat Man at the end of *The Maltese Falcon*, "He's not a fall guy unless he's a cinch to take the fall." The modern fall guy takes the blame, or "carries the can," for someone else's misconduct or blunder.

The premise here is that our main character is going to be a scapegoat. Why and how he becomes one is the thrust of the narrative of this particular short film. We have to choose a person and a situation—but not necessarily a situation that will telegraph the fate of the main character to the audience. Perhaps the most critical task here is to create a situation that will make the outcome (that the character will become the fall guy) logical and that will create a character with whose plight we can empathize.

Our story will be a fantasy about an IRS bureaucrat who decides that he has had enough of saying no to the taxpayer, and that from now on he will say yes. He is the man in charge of income tax refunds. When the IRS communicates to the Treasury Department that it needs more money for refunds, the Treasury official replies that the Treasury had been about to ask the IRS for money (of course, the Internal Revenue Service essentially collects money for the Treasury). The official at the Treasury, also a bureaucrat, will not be able to report to his superior that he has the necessary money; the Treasury bureaucrat's mission is not accomplished. Will he be the fall guy for the IRS? The story can unfold in a few ways, but in any case, the bureaucrat at the Treasury should be the fall guy. Clearly, the bureaucrat at the IRS is someone we all want to succeed.

This bureaucratic fantasy should focus on the fall guy at the Treasury, and we should on one level feel satisfaction at the fact that we can identify with and appreciate the prospect of greater refunds. In this story, the protagonist's fate fulfills the audience's fantasy—to get a refund—and, consequently, the audience will accept not only the premise but also the fate of the fall guy.

The Anecdote

An anecdote, whether told by a friend or picked up in a newspaper, can be an excellent starting point for a screen story. The following is an example of such an anecdote.

This particular anecdote does not have much narrative or a main character, the way our earlier source material did. It does, however contain a powerful irony: the subjugation, under the name of religion, of indigenous people. This is not a unique story, since it could easily be used to describe the early incursions of Western European powers into North and South America. In a sense, it is one of the major patterns of colonialism. Our challenge as writers is to use this powerful fact and metaphor and make it the spine of a short film story. Our approach can be realistic, dramatized, or animated. For the sake of providing an example of a different type from those used earlier, we will approach this anecdote with the goal of creating a story suitable for animation.

In order to focus on the concept of a moment of prayer turning into subjugation, we need to decide on a narrative and a character. We also need to make the point that at a certain time, blacks owned the land and were in power in South Africa. If possible, we should avoid the horrible cliché of traders giving gifts to the natives in exchange for property; to evoke Manhattan being purchased for a handful of trinkets can undermine the originality of our approach.

We suggest a story focusing on the meaning of prayer, in particular a specific prayer with meaning across different cultural groups and various historical periods. We can choose from prayers thanking the deity for the harvest or for the birth of a child, prayers for a death, or prayers asking or inviting the deity to provide. In our story approach, we will focus on prayers for a bountiful harvest. This will unify the story around prayer. It will also allow us to spotlight the land, the need to feed the local population, and the power structure in the area.

We will focus on a tribe, with a king and a shaman. The characters are black. In our story, a king shows his son how to lead his people to a bountiful harvest. The king will speak of the need for rain, for peace with one's neighbors, and for sons and daughters to reap the harvest. Each scene focuses on an aspect of this prayer—for rain, for peace, for sons and daughters. Each scene ends with success, and in it the point should be made that the son in each scene is the king in the next. In this way, continuity over time suggests success.

◆ ◆ ◆

15

SHORT REVIEW : ELEMENTS OF FILM

Contemporary film theory — at least part of it — is increasingly concerned with how a film is put together. What are the irreducible parts or elements? How do they relate to each other? How do they work on an audience?

Ideally, a movie is very simple: you are watching something and listening to something. Abstractly what you watch are: color, shape, form, and movement. What you listen to are: language and sound, with rhythms, harmonies, and melodies.Concretely we watch people, either alone or together, objects, scenery, and events. We listen to monologues and conversations, narration, sound effects, music and silence. Simple eh? Successful film artistically or financially or both, simply combine all these elements, concrete and abstract into a pleasing pattern. But the whole question is what makes one pattern pleasing and another not? What sells?

The industry moguls certainly do not know, at least, in the long run. Film business is notoriously mercurial and even the best efforts of conglomerate accountants and vice-presidents have not been able to bring and stability to it.What we do know now, as in the seventies, is that the value of a film does not lie so much in its particular genre but with elements that historically have been associated with that genre that can be abstracted and grafted onto another subject entirely.

Caper films such as *Butch Cassidy and the Sundance Kid, The Sting, Five Easy Pieces, Scarecrow, The Chase, The Fugitive* did not last as pure genre much past 1975 simply because filmmakers learned to use the elements of suspense and myth inherent in those genres in other types of films.

The hybrids had more going for them. Example, *French Connection* has a superb chase in it. It has also the elements of caper. It was a Buddy film in part, but primarily it was copy story.

All the President's Men was not just a movie about politics. It was an intellectual chase (inexorable because we know the aftermath). A bit of a caper, with touches of docudrama, and an undercurrent of Buddy. Literary texts used to list the basic elements of a novel as plot, character, setting, theme and style. This five (5) point model remains useful for an analysis of the conscious motivation of the film. Psychologically, film may work in a much more complex manner — but practically for both the filmmaker and film viewer — movies remain stories, stories about people, in certain locations, that present a number of ideas, and do so in a more or less recognizable aesthetic manner.

A. STORY

More than anything else, a good story is the basis for most successful films, and it is told in the most conventional manner despite what you may have heard about the new artistic freedom in Hollywood. (The following Tagalog films succeeded in a way because of their stories: *Pakawalan Mo Ako, Kung Mangarap Ka't Magising, Tinimbang Ka....*)

A good story has a very clear beginning, middle and end. It is divided into fairly equal thirds. It moves in a good order from exposition through development, to denouement and conclusion. It is tightly knit (then what happened? And then? And then?), but it often leaves space for other profitable enterprises, such as character and setting. The best way to organize the telling of a story is through proper balance of suspense and action. Alfred Hitchcock was fond of defining suspense as the "the opposite of surprise."

Surprise: when something happens and you don't expect it.

Suspense: when you expect it and it doesn't happen.

Any story upon which the element of surprise, action and suspense can be superimposed is a candidate for success in the

Hollywood format or any format for that matter. Often, the suspense/ action balance can be adjusted after the film is shot.

Steven Spielberg owes much of his success to an instinctive understanding of this process n Jaws (also to Verna Field's excellent help in editing). In both *Jaws* and *Close Encounters*, Spielberg is confronted with rather thin stories. Not a lot happens either. The films work because of what does not happen. In *Jaws*, the shark enters the bay, but it does not eat the children. In *Close Encounters*, the aliens give the signal but their spaceships do not land until the end of the movie. Spielberg knows very well how to build on these non-events by keeping the nervous tension of the characters at a high level from the beginning. He even shoots new footage which appears at the opening of the film *Close Encounters*. There is no reason for a sandstorm in the desert to be there when Lacombe goes to investigate the mysteriously returned airplanes. No reason, except that the sandstorm is noisy, tense, dangerous.

B. CHARACTER

The general run of American films is strongly plot-oriented, however, the best American movies depend heavily on character for the full effect, even at the expense of storyline. (N.B. Directors who are more interested in character than action: Woody Allen, John Cassavetes, Robert Altman, Francis Coppola, Paul Mazursky, Lino Brocka, Danny Zialcita, Ishmael Bernal.) he suspense/action style was so widespread in the 70's; clearly Spielberg supplied the action in that period, even when the action was not necessarily there. Films relied heavily on ACTORS to bring the action alive.

Example, *French Connection* could not have worked without Gene Hackman. *Star Wars* found an appropriate crux in Alec Guinness Obi-Wan Kenobi and the resonant voice dubbed after shooting of James Earl Jones as Darth Vader.

Without Richard Dreyfuss and Robert Shaw (to a lesser extent Roy Scheider) Jaws would not have been the film it was, and Dreyfuss once more with Francois Truffaut breathed life into *Close Encounters*.

In the films just mentioned, it is the actor, the star, who brings character to the role. In films which are in the first place oriented towards character, the material is there to begin with like *Ordinary People*, *Kramer vs Kramer*. On the other hand, there were films, *The Godfather* for example, that made stars of a number of hitherto unknown actors, because the roles themselves had power: Al Pacino, Robert de Niro, James Caan, Diane Keaton.

People may go to the movies for the visceral excitement of professionally paced action, but they become moviegoers because of the people they see on the screen. They come back to see these beautiful people.

C. SETTING

Setting is probably the most important in film that any other art. Moreover, it increases in importance with each passing year. People do go to movies to see places they have not been, whether it is another galaxy, Basilan, Tawi-Tawi, or Rio de Janeiro. (Albeit, they also like to see places they have been.)

The indoor movies, once a staple of the studios, prisoners of their huge, expensive lights, often seems cramped and claustrophobic.

But setting alone can't make a commercially successful film (ex. *Cherry Blossoms*, *Miss X*, *Pinoy Matador*). They are all essentially travelogues. Location work adds immeasurably to a film with other things going for it. For example, *Maynila Sa Mga Kuko Ng Liwanag*, *Insiang*, *Cruising*, *Julia*, *The Boys from Brazil* have a grit and texture that they would not have had on a studio set. William Friedkin's underrated *Sorcerer* might not have been worth the $20 million it cost to make, but it certainly did provide an interesting trip. Same with *Apocalypse Now*.

Since studios per se have been largely freed from reproducing New York streets and plantation mansions, they are now able to devote their energies to the construction of fantasies, like *Star Wars*, *Alien*. Hence there is a rise of science fiction (Sci-Fi) like the *Red Planet*, and wonderfully symbolic and mechanical *James Bond* interiors. Setting is not a matter of locale alone. People are also fascinated by the way things work. One of the main pleasures of the caper films is figuring out how the puzzle will be solved. As the old TV caper series *Mission Impossible* used to phrase it at the beginning of every show: "Your mission, should you choose to accept it, is…". Here are the premises, what's the solution.

Francois Truffaut thinks one of the strengths of American movies has been — they showed how working people's jobs are done — as a pedagogical tool, film can explain how to perform a task better than a book, better than a record, and better than a still photograph. This epistemological value should be recognized in fictional entertainment too.

D. THEME

Theme is, perhaps surprisingly, a salable commodity. People go to adventure films, to women's films, to mid-life crisis movies, to youth films etc., at least partially for what those films have to say — MESSAGE.

Example *Network* was not a success because of Paddy Chayeksky's heaty dialogue. It was not Faye Dunaway or Bill Holden that linked them up around the block — it was the subject, television and the attitude the film expressed toward it. *Network* did not make the point very clearly, but people wanted to hear any critique of TV. Same is with *Being There*, the last film of Peter Sellers. *All The President's Men* attracted viewers mainly because it helped explain how Watergate had happened and people wanted to hear it too. There had been a market of films about the way we live, and the more it was catered to, the larger it would grow.

Movies have always been prized by critics and general audiences alike for the strong mythic base on which they are built. That is the chief reason for the perennial popularity of genres like the western, the gangster, and the detective story. (Tagalog films: Ramon Revilla's "true to life" stories like *Nardong Putik*, *Tiagong Akyat*, etc.). All films mean something; whether or not the filmmaker intends it. Interpretation — supplying meaning — is the job of the consumers as well as producers.

The thematic spectrum runs from the direct and relatively simple lessons of realistic films that describe the way we live now (*Ordinary People*, *Kramer vs. Kramer*, *And Justice for All*, *Pakawalan Mo Ako*, *Insiang*) to the more complex and amorphous significance of mythological genres (such as *Rocky*, *F.I.S.T.*, Fernando Poe's *Ang Panday*, *Santiago*). Far more being an intellectual's preoccupation, theme is the necessary skeleton on which action, character and setting are arranged. If the bare bones are not there, audiences will know it (like *Burgis*). Occasionally, a film enjoys a successful run simply because it carries with it the aura of "meaningfulness". American films that mean to be "serious" are often about outcasts or cripple (*Coming Home*, *The Deer Hunter*, *The Other Side of the Mountain*, *Inside Moves*, *Tinimbang Ka...*). Partly, audiences are attracted because such movies appeal to voyeurism and maudlin sentimentality, but basically people are interested in such downbeat films because seeing them becomes an act of moral commitment.

E. STYLE

This last of the five elements of the cinematic equation is the least defensible. Only trained observers, mass communication and communication arts students, look for it or appreciate it. If it is blatantly evident, it is usually done in bad faith, and audiences react with sensible contempt (e.g. Celso Ad Castillo's *Uhaw na Dagat*).

In European Films, style usually plays a notably more significant part than in American films. Since European films are on the whole much more personal communications, the tone of voice of the author is an important element in the grand design. You can easily spot a Bergman film, a Fellini, a Godard or Bertolucci. American films, however, can't rely on this established, intimate relationship between filmmaker and film viewer. American films exist in the context of movies as powerful mass entertainment, so that personal style, when it makes itself evident, often seems intrusive. In terms of American movies, style is all too often defined as the residue that remains after action and character, setting and ideas have been extracted.

Some American filmmakers are still enamored by the European approach despite its inapplicability to the American situation. Most egregious recent example of this falsely placed faith has been Allen's Interiors. Same can be said of Ishmael Bernal, who took up filmmaking in India, who tries to inject into his film a style that is too Indian, i.e. slow paced, long pauses, static camera, etc. *Nunal Sa Tubig* flopped because of this and to a lesser degree, *City After Dark*, which was too episodic in treatment.

F. SEX and MUSIC

To these five classic elements we should add two others, each of which is something more than a gimmick, but less than a basic component of the construction: SEX and MUSIC. They are hardly necessary and sufficient like the five from which films are built, but they can often save a "borderline case" film. There is a strong element of voyeurism to the film experience, so a judicious nude scene here and there can mean the margin between profit and less, especially when feature films are in direct competition with television. Even when a film contains no explicit sex, the very presence of actors and actresses often work to provide a sexual subtext.

MUSIC, on the other hand, may seem exterior to the film itself. Yet, it is the mortar that fills in the cracks, even sometimes when they are large enough to push a dolly through. Prove it by turning down the sound of your TV. More often than not, it is not the image that moves us, but the musical ground case that tells us what to think and how to feel about that image.

In conclusion, we can say that in American films, technique has been refined to a high state.

◆ ◆ ◆

16

TROUBLESHOOTING

Sorting the shit from the shinola is a talent every writer needs but few do it well, either through lack of objectivity, or knowledge of how to go about it, or both. Writers constantly argue the merits of lost causes and dead ends within their scripts, straining to shoehorn them into an unyielding framework because they're so in love with their ideas, or they really think it all fits together. Writing, particularly scriptwriting, is all about murdering your loved ones in the service of greater causes – drama and plot. Get used to it and get over yourself.

Script Appraisals

It helps if you know what script readers are looking for before you submit your work for consideration. If you have doubts (and you probably should), consider investing in a script appraisal. As I said, a 6-10 page report costs around Rs. 60 - Rs.100 but you'll usually find it's money well spent. I use the following appraisal checklist:

- Is it clear?
- Focused?
- Well structured?
- Written with style?
- Concept intriguing?
- Marketable?
- Cinematic or televisual?
- For what audience?

- Where does attention wane?
- Is protagonist dynamic/sympathetic?
- Clear needs/wants/goals/problems?
- Character development/interaction?
- Enough tension/conflict?
- Memorable dialogue?
- Twists and switches?
- Strong ending?
- What has protagonist learned?
- What works?
- What stinks?
- Conclusion

These points are broadly similar to those addressed by script readers and they also serve as useful guidelines when redrafting. A tip: complete your script to the best of your ability before having it appraised. If you know it has flaws, why pay to have someone else tell you?

Ten Common Problems

1. Most scripts do not have a sense of the audience/reader. They're not speaking to, or engaging the reader; there's no sense of who it's being aimed at or made for. Also, they're not written in such a way you feel the audience will 'get it' – there's no sense of clear purpose, no sense the reader feels communicated with. It's down to a basic problem of communication and this first problem encapsulates all of the other variations.

2. There's no personality coming through. It doesn't matter whether the script is well crafted, the writer has just spent time solving problems at the expense of personality. It's anonymous. Again, this is a problem of engagement.

3. There's no focused aim for the main character(s) – what do they want? There may be a vague feeling of a problem, like a marriage breakdown etc., but it's not focused. Writers fail to narrow the focus to the final part of the script that gets to the thing that solves the Hero's problem.

4. Too long spent setting up. Characters spend a long time talking about problems but too little time doing anything about them.

5. Individual scenes tend to tell rather than show.They need to be more focused and have personality and style.There's no focusing down to the essence of the scene, so that we can be shown rather than told.

6. The writer doesn't spend long enough developing character. Characters are the heart of the script.They tend to be either too positive or too negative, not complex enough. Writers should consider themselves students of people.

7. Far too much talky dialogue. If characters are endlessly talking, how is the scene going to work visually?

8. Flat writing style. The writing style has to engage the reader.There are too many nouns and adjectives used, and nowhere near enough strong verbs.

9. No theme. What's the point of it if the reader can't discern a theme? Why do it at all?

10. No difference.Writers must ask themselves the question, 'why is this different?'Too often it's just not in any way new.And if you know it's not new, then at least ask yourself, 'what am I bringing to it?'

Ten Handy Hints

1. Make obstacles for your main character. Lots of little ones – toothache, lost hair grip etc. which must be resolved. Build obstacles to delay the satisfaction of the audience.

2. Write a treatment first.There is no definitive idea of what constitutes a treatment; the terms 'treatment,''outline' and 'synopsis' are interchangeable, although the longer it is, the more likely it is to be called a treatment. And you must give the ending! A treatment helps you to clarify your thoughts. It's difficult, but very important. Start with a short pitch of 25 words or less. Films make their money on TV and video. Make it saleable to TV and condensable to a short entry in the *TV Times*: Someone wants ______, but is prevented from getting it by ________.Then write a short synopsis giving the problem, how the protagonist goes about solving it and how it all ends up – the basic three acts. Elaborate and enlarge on that for the treatment. The treatment must be readable and must flow. Use conjunctions: moreover, meanwhile, on the other side of town and so on.

3. Format is very important.Think about it like a date: you prepare yourself by showering, grooming, dressing well, looking your best.You make the effort to show yourself in the best possible light. If you don't, your date will be unimpressed. It's the same with format. If your script format is wrong, your story may not have attention paid to it. And yes, you must use 12 point Courier. Format is vital, it's part of your marketing.

4. Write your first draft quickly, then rewrite slowly.

5. Put it aside for a few months.You need that distance. Or, have lots of people look at it. Show it to friends. Give them a list of questions – tell them to stop at page 40, then write down who is the main character, what do they want, what are their problems, how are they going about solving them? Find out if you are communicating with and engaging the reader.

6. Deal with every problem. There's no such thing as a problem you can sweep under the carpet. If there's a hint of a problem, it will be magnified throughout the process, and certainly found out by a reader.

7. When you've finished your script, find a producer or producers who seem to share your sensibility. Join organisations that can help you – the NPA and the SW, definitely.

8. Never send your script out cold; always use an approach letter, or a phone call.

9. Build relationships, network etc. Be a collaborator. The industry wants people they can work with. All scripts need rewriting. Compromises have to be made.

10. When you send out your scripts, use thick envelopes. It's amazing how many arrive tatty or shredded because the writer has used thin, flimsy envelopes. Padded envelopes are best.

Five Common Problems

1. Writing a story where the hero does not have clearly defined wants and needs. 95% of stories fail because of this.

2. Writing a story which is not commercially viable.

3. Presenting a screenplay in incorrect format.

4. Writing a story where there is no ghost or backstory, or writing a story where the hero overcomes the ghost too easily.

5. Writing a story containing characters the audience cannot identify with.

The core problems identified by Charles and Elliot will be familiar to all script readers. Use their advice and the following checklist to help diagnose and solve your script's problems.

Troubleshooting 10-Point Checklist

1. Does your protagonist have clearly defined motivations and goals: needs, desires, fears, ghost, problems? Have you communicated to the reader who the protagonist is, what he wants, how he plans to achieve his goals and what's standing in his way?

2. Do your characters exist in their own world as complex, three-dimensional, credible people with whom the reader can identify? If they're not alive in your mind they won't be alive in the reader's. What are their backstories? Do you know your characters well enough?

3. Who is your audience? What is the genre? How would you market the finished film? Does your script have commercial appeal, or an everyman quality? Do you know whether it's high-concept (with such a strong premise that audiences will go and see it for that reason alone), or low/soft-concept (depends more on the quality of the end product to attract its audience, and therefore more risky for financiers)? Why would anyone pay to watch this film? Why would anyone pay to fund this film?

4. What is the point of your script? What makes it different; what's worth the time, effort and paper? What is the theme – what is it really about? Are you communicating this effectively? Do you know yourself – could you state the theme as well as the premise if asked? Are you saying something because you're desperate to say it or because you think it's commercial?

5. Is your script coherent and integrated, or a Frankensteinian monster of loosely-assembled parts? Do you have enough ideas, characters and sub-plots to sustain a 90-120 page script? Have you paid enough attention to structure? Does your opening hit the ground running and hook the reader? What are your end-of-act plot points? Is there a mid-point? Does your ending deliver, and tie all the plot strands? Are you engaging the reader and holding interest throughout? Are you building tension, accelerating the pace, increasing the frequency and difficulty of obstaclcs your protagonist faces? Or does interest wane, the pace sag and the script run out of steam? Are you capable of objectivity when self-analysing?

6. Is your writing style stylish enough? Are you transmitting your story visually into the mind of the reader (showing), or indulging in bland reportage (telling)? Remember that in screenwriting, less is definitely more. Is your scene description pared down, fast paced and specific or mean- dering, hyperbolic and general?

7. Does your protagonist spend enough time in active pursuit of goals and solving problems or too much time talking? Readers engage with characters through actions first and dialogue a distant second. Is there enough at stake? Is your protagonist in enough danger? Is he on the edge? True character is revealed only in adversity. What does he stand to lose – a game of poker, a round of golf or loved ones, career, reputation, life? Is his goal difficult, plausible and important enough? Is the reader given a sense of gravitas or couldn't care less?

8. Have you laid out your script in the correct format? Is it too long or too short? Is it full of typos, spelling and/or grammatical errors, strange punctuation? These elements are not negotiable. Sending out a badly formatted or presented script is an excuse for a reader to put a cross against your name. It's a crime of stupidity. You may as well include your own pre-written rejection slip.

9. Have you remembered that scripts are about parallel action? Several things are happening to several people at once. Are you showing this by cutting back and forth between them, often? Are your scenes short and sweet enough to allow the script to flow or do you concentrate on one character's plot line for too long at a time?

10. Does your script contain that synergy of concept, execution, character and incident that elevates it from a televisual to a cinematic experience? Would the film of your script cry out to be viewed in a cinema or would it lose nothing if shown on a TV screen? Have you gone to the extremes with your characters, situations and style? Is your canvas large enough, or is it television masquerading as film?

◆ ◆ ◆

17

FILM SCRIPT TERMINOLOGY

The best way to learn about screenplays is to read a variety of film scripts.But before you can understand everything you read you need to know about basic script terminology. Most of the following applies to both film scripts and television scripts.

TRANSITIONS

The basic transitions from one scene to another are:

- **cuts** - instantaneous changes from one scene to the next
- **lap-dissolves,** also called **dissolves** - where two scenes momentarily overlap during a transition from one to the other
- **fade-out** and **fade-in** - fade-out consists of a two-or three-second transition from a picture to black and silence; and, of course, a fadein is the opposite

Traditionally, screenplays (dramatic film scripts) start with *fade in* and close with *fade out.* Fade-ins and fade-outs within the production can signal a major change or division within the story structure, such as a passage of time.

An **insert shot** is a close-up of something within the scene. For example, after a man looks at his watch, you might see a cut to close-up of the watch where you can clearly see the time.

A **cutaway** is a related shot that is "away" from the basic scene. For example, during a basketball game you might "cut away" from the action on the floor to a shot of a fan in the stands eating a hot dog.

Script Terms and Abbreviations

Although scriptwriters sometimes feel an urge to indicate camera shots and angles on a script, as we've previously suggested, this is an area that's best left to the judgment of the director.

Even so, in dramatic scripts you will often see the terms *camera finds* indicate the camera moves in on a particular portion of a scene; *camera goes with* to indicate the camera moves with a person or object; *reverse angle* to indicate a near 180-degree shift in camera position; and *shot widens* to signal a zoom or dolly back.

When the entire camera is moved toward or away from the subject, it's referred to as a **dolly.**

A **zoom,** which is an optical version of a dolly, achieves somewhat the same effect. Even so, many Directors of Photography feel that compared to a dolly, a zoom is somewhat artificial looking.

To indicate either one, a script notation might say, "camera zooms in for close-up of John," or "camera zooms out to show that John is not alone."

When a lateral move is needed, the term is **truck.**

In film, both the dolly and truck movement are often referred to as **tracking shots.** Sometimes you also see the term **moving shot** to indicate that the camera moves in some way during the course of a scene.

Shot designations for films include:

Long shot (LS) or **full shot (FS).** With people, this is a shot from the top of their heads to at least their feet.

A **medium shot (MS)** is normally a shot from the waist up.

A **medium close-up (MCU)** is a shot cropped between the shoulders and the belt line.

A close-up **(CU)** is the most desirable to catch changing facial expressions, which are important to following a conversation.

Extreme close-ups **(XCUs)** are reserved for dramatic impact. The XCU shot may show just the eyes of an individual.

All of these designations can also apply to objects, as in

"close-up of toaster shows toast popping up."

A **boom shot, jib shot,** or **crane shot** refer to high-angle shots, sometimes with the camera moving.

An **establishing shot** is a wide shot (WS) or a long shot (LS). This type of shot gives an audience a basic orientation to the geography of a scene — who is where — after which there should be cuts to closer shots. Thereafter, establishing shots can be momentarily used as reminders or updates on scene changes where people have moved in relation to each other, etc. In this context they are called **reestablishing shots.**

A **master shot** is similar to an establishing shot, but this term is generally reserved for the special needs of film. Once the master shot action is filmed the scene is generally shot over again from different camera positions so that there are shots (especially close-ups) of each actor. Dialogue and actor reactions are repeated each time the camera is repositioned.

These scenes are referred to as **coverage.** Often, numerous **takes** (filmed sequences from the different camera positions in the coverage) are required before a director is satisfied.

During **editing** all of the film footage will be assembled to make it appear that there is a continuous flow of action. To do this the editor must smoothly cut together the footage from the numerous takes.

Actors must repeat everything over again in exactly the same way for each take in the coverage. This means they must use the same energy level with the same actions at the exact points in their dialogue. This is essential in being able to later unobtrusively cut together the various takes during editing to create a smooth, unbroken flow of action.

A **two-shot** or **three-shot** (also 2-S and 3-S) designates a shot of two or three people in one scene.

The term **subjective shot** indicates that the audience (camera) will see what the character sees. Often it indicates a handheld camera shot that moves in a walking or running motion while following an actor. Subjective camera shots can add drama and frenzy to chase scenes.

Camera angles are also sometimes indicated on scripts. Included are bird's eye view, high angle (photo on left), eye-level, and low angle shots.

A **canted shot** or a **Dutch angle** shot (on the right) is tilted 25 to 45 degrees to one side, causing horizontal lines be at an angle.

In addition to these basic script terms, there are a number of other abbreviations used in script writing.

• **EXT** and **INT** designations are commonly listed in film scripts to indicate exterior and interior settings. (Note script below).

• **VO (voice over)** refers to narration heard over a scene. It can also refer to narration heard at a higher level than a source of music or background sound.

• **POV (point of view)**. Screenplays will sometimes note that a shot will be seen from the point of view of a particular actor.

• **OS (shot-over-the-shoulder shot)**. The scene shows the back of one person's head and possibly one shoulder.

• **SFX (special effects)**. These may be audio special effects or visual effects — effects that alter reality and are created in the postproduction and editing phases.

◆ ◆ ◆

18

A SCREENWRITING GLOSSARY

A

• **ACTION DESCRIPTION:** the overt, physical actions that happen on screen, such as "He falls down the stairs" or "She pulls a gun, hands shaking."

• **ACTOR:** a gifted individual who has studied the craft of acting in order to portray roles in performances of dramatic literaure.

• **ALTER-EGO:** a substitute "self" for a writer, usually a protagonist in the writer's story.

• **AMBIENCE:** overall quality of mood, tone, atmosphere in a film.

• **ANTAGONIST:** a character that puts barriers and reversals in the way of a protagonist's progress or objective.

• **ARCHETYPE:** a universal character modeled upon those that have been appearing in stories since the time of our ancient ancestors.

• **ASSISTANT DIRECTOR:** a film crew member whose job it is to manage the set protocols and keep the film shoot on schedule.

• **ATMOSPHERE:** the dominant mood or emotional tone of a film.

• **AUDIENCE EXPECTATION:** particular elements of a film genre which the audience consciously or unconsciously expects to see.

B

• **BARRIER:** a first act obstacle in the way of a protagonist's objective.

• **BEAT:** a unit of action within a scene or act that marks subtle shifts in the direction or control of the plot action.

• **BOOK-ENDING:** a framing device within which a main plot line is presented as being told or read to another, often embellished by the use of a voice-over narration throughout the film.

• **BUDDY FILM:** a popular movie genre in which two protagonists (often confidantes) are in pursuit of the same objective (willingly or unwillingly) and sometimes trade off as catalysts to one another.

C

• **CAMERA ANGLE:** the angle from which a shot is to be taken (e.g., a close-up angle is a shot that should be made from a close proximity to the subject, either through tighter lens focusing or by the camera being placed physically closer to the action).

• **CAMERA MOVE:** an action description in a screenplay that stipulates a specific move of the camera (such as "CAMERA PANS a crowded supermarket at rush hour.")

• **CAST:** the actors who portray the characters in a performance of dramatic literature.

• **CATALYST (CATALYTIC):** a character, event, or circumstances which force a protagonist into a quest or achieving of an objective.

• **CATHARSIS:** the emotional effect upon an audience resulting from a re-living or re-experiencing of a remembered emotion

• **CAUSAL PREDICTION:** an audience's unconscious forecasting of what will happen in a standard plot based on certain known causes and effects (e.g., boy meets girl, boy loses girl, causal prediction=boy gets girl).

• **CAUSE-AND-EFFECT:** a linear sequence of events that logically progress from one to the other, with the prior action "causing" the latter to happen. (E.g., a person witnesses a murder, causing the effect of the murderer stalking the witness.)

• **CENTRAL QUESTION:** the question that arises in the audience's mind as they are introduced to a protagonist within a set of given circumstances that propel the character into some kind of action.

• **CHARACTER:** a person, animal, or spiritual entity that figures importantly in the telling of a story.

• **CHARACTER DEVELOPMENT:** the gradual revelation of information about a character that the audience needs to know in order to understand the character's motivations and intent.

• **CHARACTER DIATRIBE:** Screenwriter Steve Tesich's writing technique for imagining characters and conflicts in the early genesis of a screenplay.

• **CHARACTER NAME:** the name of the character speaking, appearing just above the dialogue line, in all caps and centered within the dialogue margins.

• **CHARACTERIZATION:** an actor's interpretation of a role in a performance of dramatic literature.

• **CINEMATIC LANGUAGE:** a "language" of images (visual and aural) that tell story without the use of words.

• **CLIMAX:** the point of highest intensity, catharsis, and suspense just before a resolution.

• **COMMEDIA DEL ARTE:** popular comedies performed in the streets of Italy during the 16th-18th centuries, using stock characters or archetypes in universal story lines and structures.

• **COMPELLING MOVEMENT:** plot action imbued with the kind of forceful energy that pushes the plot forward, forcing the story line to move toward a climax and resolution.

• **COMPLICATION:** an action point that is introduced early in the film with no obvious effect or importance until later, when it becomes the unexpected source of difficulties or solutions to the protagonist's objective.

• **COMPOSITE:** a character that is based upon more than one person or personality in a writer's life or imagination.

• **CONFIDANTE:** a character who shares secrets, personal information, or discussions of intimate or internal conflicts with another.

• **CONFLICT:** opposition, controversy, struggle, contradiction, or antipathy between a character and him/herself, his/her situation, another character, society, or spiritual belief.

• **CONTRAST:** the emphasized difference between story elements pointed up by a juxtaposition of those elements to one another.

• **CREW:** the staff members of a film production

• **CROSS-GENRE:** two genres combined to create a more rich and complex movie.

• **CUT:** the transitional movement on screen from once scene or shot to the next.

• **CUTAWAY:** a quick transition to another secondary shot (often of some lesser or ironic element of the setting) and back to the main shot.

D

• **DENOUEMENT:** the final resolution to an intricate plot.

• **DESIGNER:** an artist who designs some element of the look or sound of a film.

• **DEVELOPMENT:** a) the gradual growth of a screenplay from germinal idea to fleshed out plot to final script; b) the breakdown, budgeting, and capitalization stage of bringing a screenplay into production (re-writes are often involved in the development stage.)

• **DIALOGUE:** the façade of heard language that reveals the subtextual struggles going on between characters.

• **DIMENSIONALITY:** richness of atmosphere or texture added to a film by means of smaller elements such as supporting characters, background actions or dialogue, or small details of design.

• **DIRECTOR:** the main orchestrator of the various creative activities that go into film production, the director collaborates with and guides designers, editors, cinematographers, technicians, and actors in their interpretation of the script within a single organic vision.

• **DISTRIBUTOR:** the entity or company who distributes a completed film to exhibitors

• **DRAMATIC ACTION:** the subtextual undercurrents and reciprocal actions that occur beneath the dialogue and physical actions of a screenplay.

E

• **EDITOR:** the technician who "cuts" and assembles a movie from raw footage shot during principal photography, cutting it into a completed film with an eye to pacing, rhythm, suspense and cinematic image storytelling.

• **ELEMENTS:** the smaller parts of a movie that must be written and noted during the breakdown and budgeting process (e.g., cast, set pieces, vehicles, music, etc.).

• **ENVIRONMENTAL FACTS:** the geographical location, time of year, season, day, period of history, and economic, political, social, moral, or religious environment of the special world of the screenplay.

• **ESTIMATOR:** an accountant or production manager who estimates the cost of making a movie from a screenplay.

• **EXPOSITION:** the revelation of previous action to a story (or earlier action in a script) that must be imbued with present dramatic action and an intimation of a future development.

F

• **FILMMAKING:** the act of recording a performance on film

• **FLASHBACK:** a transition from a scene to one that has taken place prior to it.

• **FORESHADOWING:** a metaphoric or symbolic indication of something to come.

• **FORMAT:** the specific layout, typeface, point size, and punctuation required by the film industry for professional screenplays.

G

• **GENRE:** a type of film for which audience have a set of particular expectations in regard to plot, style, tone, outcome, and theme.

• **GIVEN CIRCUMSTANCES:** the environmental facts, previous action, and polar attitudes of a dramatic story.

I

• **INTENT:** the subtextual objective of a character

J

• **JEOPARDY:** a condition of possible physical or emotional danger or suffering of a character or characters that raises the stakes of a plot.

L

• **LEGEND:** written information superimposed on an image or blank screen (e.g., "Long ago, in a galaxy far away…"

• **LINEAR STRUCTURE:** a plot structure that runs in a chronological or logical cause-and-effect sequence.

• **LOCATION MANAGER:** a film crew worker who scouts, contracts, and manages the location sets (as opposed to studio sets) for film productions. Locations are usually real places used as found sets with a minimum of set dressing or construction.

• **LOG LINE:** an extremely short description of the plot, characters, theme, and genre of a screenplay used to pitch or synopsize scripts during the development stage.

M

• **MARKETING DIRECTOR:** the project manager in charge of determining how best to promote and distribute a movie to the public.

• **MENTOR CHARACTER:** a character that helps a protagonist in achieving his or her objective; often, they serve as catalysts and may also articulate the theme of the story.

• **MID POINT SCENE:** a plot point that seems to divide the second act of a story in half, usually serving to emphasize or articulate the larger theme or message of the story.

• **MONTAGE:** a sequence of images or short scenes that reveal story points or important exposition in an encapsulated manner.

• **MOTIF:** a recurring image, sound, line, action or other element that makes a symbolic, allegorical, metaphoric or thematic point in a movie.

• **MOTIVATION: a)** the situation, reasoning, or driving compulsion behind a character's intent; **b)** the character background or situational factors that actors analyze to "motivate" their performance of a role.

• **MOVIE:** a dramatic performance that is recorded as a moving image, whether on film or videotape.

• **MYTH:** a story that has been told and re-told for centuries and which seems rooted in universal human experiences that people want to re-experience in new forms again and again.

• **MYTHIC ELEMENT:** a story element that seems taken from myth.

O

• **OBJECTIVE:** the goal or desire of a protagonist(s).

• **OBSTACLE:** a barrier or reversal that presents a challenge to a protagonist's achievement of an objective.

• **OMNISCIENT (OMNISCIENCE):** storytelling that is told from an all-knowing, all-seeing point of view.

• **ONE-LINE DESCRIPTION:** a very brief one-sentence description of what happens in a scene.

• **ORGANIC STRUCTURE:** a writing structure in which all of story elements relate to one another and to the whole in a complete and unified manner so as to make overall emotional or thematic sense to the reader or audience.

• **OUT OF CONTINUITY:** out of chronological or linear order (used to describe the way in which movie scenes are shot during principal photography).

• **OUTCOME:** the resolution of a story in terms of the protagonist's objective.

P

• **PACE:** the intensity, rhythm or speed (or lack thereof) of a story's plot action.

• **PAGE COUNT:** the number of eighths of a page of script content that takes place in one setting, used to calculate the amount of time it will take to shoot a script.

• **PARENTHETICAL:** one or two words that qualify the tone of a dialogue line when it is not clear from the subtext or context of the line how it should be played; a parenthetical is placed in parentheses just above the dialogue line and indented.

• **PERIOD:** an historical time and place that serves as the setting or "special world" of a screenplay story.

• **PITCH:** a brief verbal description of a screenplay idea or script (often based on a written logline) usually told by a writer, director, or producer to someone who is interested in buying, financing, or developing a story idea or script.

• **PLAY:** dramatic literature that is performed live as if happening in the present moment, in front of a live audience.

• **PLOT ACTION:** the physical actions and story points that propel a story through to a climax and resolution.

• **PLOT PAY-OFF:** the consequence or outcome of a plot point or story element that is set-up earlier in a screenplay.

• **PLOT POINT (OR ACTION POINT):** a significant or overt action or moment within a plot that creates obstacles, raises the stakes, articulates theme, or complicates things for a protagonist trying to reach an objective.

• **POINT OF VIEW (POV):** the position from which an image is supposed to be seen, requiring the placing of the camera in that relationship.

• **POLAR ATTITUDE:** a character's emotional attitude or approach to other characters, to his/her situation, to society, or to him or her self.

• **POST PRODUCTION:** the phase of production that follows principal photography, in which raw footage is cut and assembled into a finished movie with added soundtrack and visual effects.

• **PRESENT ACTION:** action that takes place in the present moment as opposed to backstory.

• **PREVIOUS ACTION (BACKSTORY):** action that has taken place prior to the opening of the movie, which the audience must know in order to understand the storyline and motivations of the character.

• **PRINCIPAL PHOTOGRAPHY:** the phase of production in which all of the moving images are photographed and recorded according to the instructions of the screenplay in preparation for later editorial cutting and assembly.

• **PRODUCTION MANAGER:** the main supervisor of the crew in charge of keeping a film project on time and on budget; the PM negotiates all financial and contractual affairs for the project during pre-production, principal photography, and sometimes post production.

• **PROTAGONIST:** the main character whom the audience identifies with or cares about in a story.

Q

• **QUALITY:** the tone or characteristic nature of a story element

R

• **RECIPROCAL ACTION:** dramatic action that entails a subtextual struggle for control or mastery between two or more characters in a scene.

• **RED HERRING:** a false lead, assumed outcome or obvious solution that a writer plants in a story to fool the audience from guessing the real outcome.

• **RELATIONSHIP WEB:** the complex network of relationships emanating from the protagonist(s) and relating him/her to the significant or supporting characters within a story.

• **RESOLUTION:** the outcome of a screenplay in terms of its plot set-up and development.

• **REVERSAL:** a serious second act obstacle to a protagonist's objective

• **RHYTHM:** the quality of the pacing and speed of a script's plot action and scene sequences.

S

• **SCENE:** continuous action with or without dialogue that takes place in one setting

• **SCENE HEADING (OR SLUG LINE):** basic set description at the top of a script scene, written in all caps, providing information as to whether the scene is interior vs. exterior, day or night, and where it takes place

• **SCREENPLAY:** a form of dramatic literature used as an instruction manual for the production of a movie.

• **SCRIPT BREAKDOWN:** a) an analysis of a screenplay in which all of the production elements are reduced to lists in order to schedule and budget the production; b) a director's creative analysis of the dramatic action, reciprocal struggle, theme, and design elements of a screenplay.

• **SET:** wherever camera is in place for a shot that is being set up for shooting (or being shot) at a location or studio.

• **SETTING:** the place in which a scene happens (not to be confused with location or set)

• **SET-UP:** the premise or given circumstances laid out at the beginning of a story, just before the catalyst propels the story into its development and resolution.

• **SHOOTING SCHEDULE:** a principal photography production

schedule created by a production manager and assistant director to organize the shooting of scenes out-of-continuity in the most economical and time-saving way possible.

• **SIMULTANEITY:** the quality of having two or more things happening at once

• **SLUG LINE (OR SCENE HEADING):** basic set description at the top of a script scene, written in all caps, providing information as to whether the scene is interior vs. exterior, day or night, and where it takes place.

• **STEP OUTLINE:** a plot outline used by writers to help organize and visualize their story before writing it; a step outline consists of scene headings followed by brief one-line descriptions in sequential order.

• **STOCK CHARACTER:** an archetypal character that shows up again and again in story throughout the ages, fulfilling a universal purpose (such as a mentor character or comic foil to the protagonist)

• **STORYTELLING:** human communication that springs from a fundamental desire in people to tell each other what happened through the most expressive and immediate means possible; in dramatic storytelling, the recreation of events and people are portrayed through present action visual and oral performance.

• **SUBPLOT:** a secondary plot line that enhances a main plot and intersects with it at a crucial point in the climax.

• **SUBTEXT:** the undercurrent of emotions and polar attitude shifts that lie beneath physical action and between the lines of dialogue.

• **SUBTEXTUAL STRUGGLE:** the reciprocal action of a scene's dramatic subtext, in which two or more characters struggle for mastery or control of the moment.

• **SUPPORTING CHARACTER:** a subplot character or minor character who helps to raise the stakes for the main protagonist, or who reflects the same problems or issues of the protagonist, while providing texture or dimensionality to the setting.

• **SUSPENSE:** a state of excitement or apprehension created by the pacing and sequencing of scenes, through the raising of a protagonist's emotional or physical stakes, or through the creation of jeopardy situations for a protagonist.

T

• **TECHNICIAN:** a crew person who performs some kind of technical (as opposed to design) function (such as grips, gaffers, sound mixers, boom operators, script supervisors, etc.)

• **TELEPLAY:** a form of dramatic literature used as an instruction manual for the production of television shows.

• **TEXTURE:** a characteristic visual or tactile quality produced by certain kinds of images (such as a story that has many scenes that take place in the rain or which incorporates images drenched in rain to produce a cold and "damp" feeling in the viewer).

• **THEMATIC THREAD:** a metaphoric element, literary or cinematic device used within a film to weave an underlying message or theme throughout the story.

• **THEME:** an underlying philosophical, social or spiritual message that gives the plot meaning and elevates the story to its essential, universal human ideas.

• **THREE ACT STRUCTURE:** the beginning, middle, and end of a story, played out in linear sequence.

• **TITLE SEQUENCE:** a scene or sequence of scenes over which the title roll of the movie credits are superimposed (usually at or near the beginning of the movie).

• **TONE:** the attitude toward a subject or story that is being expressed by the writer or director of a screenplay or film (such as cynicism, hope, anger, optimism, sadness, or wonder). The resolution of a story may inform the tone of the piece in the long run, even when a different tone may have been set earlier on.

• **TRANSFORMATIONAL ARC:** the parabolic shift in polar attitudes of a character from a point A to a point B during the course of a story.

• **TRANSITION:** a direction in a screenplay that informs the filmmakers as to the quality of the cut from one scene to the next (such as "DISSOLVE TO:"); it appears flush right between the end of one scene and the beginning of the next.

• **TURNING POINT:** an action point that is a reaction to an obstacle in the way of a protagonist's objective; turning points raise the stakes, move the action in a different direction or to a different playing area, and force the protagonist to take a new or different tack.

U

- **UNIT:** a beat of reciprocal action or a resolved bit of subtextual struggle within a scene.
- **UNITY:** the way in which the components of a story relate to each other and to the story as a whole so that it makes overall emotional or thematic sense.
- **UNIVERSALITY:** a quality that transcends the subjective experience of the individual to find the universal reality of human experience.

V

- **VIDEOGRAPHY:** the recording of a performance by means of video camera and videotape.
- **VISUAL:** having to do with that which can be seen (vs. heard)
- **VISUAL EFFECT:** a special visual technique used to enhance storytelling (such as computer animation, slow motion, or time-lapse photography).
- **VOICEOVER NARRATION:** a narration heard over the images of a scene.

FADE OUT :

◆ ◆ ◆

References & Notes

Books On Screenwriting

• *Screenplay: The Foundations Of Screenwriting* (Third Edition) by Syd Field, US: Dell, 1994, Paperback, 262 pages, $13.95, ISBN 0440576474

• *The Screenwriter's Workbook* by Syd Field, US: Dell, 1984, Paperback, 211 pages, $9.95, ISBN 0440582253

• *Story: Substance, Structure, Style And The Principles Of Screenwriting* by Robert McKee, UK: Methuen, 1998, Hardback, 466 pages, £16.99, ISBN 0413715507

• *Writing Screenplays That Sell* by Michael Hauge, UK: Elm Tree, 1989, Paperback, 316 pages, £11.99, ISBN 0241126827

• *Teach Yourself Screenwriting* by Raymond G Frensham, UK: Hodder & Stoughton, 1996, Paperback, 250 pages, £6.99, ISBN 034060378X

• *Alternative Scriptwriting: Writing Beyond The Rules* by Ken Dancyger & Jeff Rush, US: Focal Press, 1991, Paperback, 212 pages, $26.95, ISBN 0240800753

• *Screenwriting 434* by Lew Hunter, US: Perigee, 1993, Paperback, 351 pages, $13.95, ISBN 039951838

• *Making A Good Script Great* by Linda Seger, US: Dodd, Mead & Company, Inc., 1987, Paperback, 204 pages, $8.95, ISBN 0396089534

• *Film Scriptwriting: A Practical Manual* (Second Edition) by Dwight V Swain & Joye R Swain, US: Focal Press, 1988, Paperback, 422 pages, ISBN 0240511905

• *How To Make Money Scriptwriting* (Second Edition) by Julian Friedmann, UK: Intellect, 2000, Paperback, 219 pages, ISBN 184150002X

• *The Complete Book Of Scriptwriting* by J Michael Straczynski, US: Writer's Digest, 1996, Hardback, 424 pages, $21.99, ISBN 0898795125

• *How To Write A Movie In 21 Days: The Inner Movie Method* by Viki King, US: Harper Perennial, 1988, Paperback, 192 pages, $11.00, ISBN

0062730665

• *Raindance Writers' Lab: Write + Sell The Hot Screenplay* by Elliot Grove, UK: Focal Press, 2001, Paperback, 240 pages plus CD-ROM, £14.95, ISBN 0240516362

Other Books Of Interest

• *The Guerilla Film-Makers Handbook* by Chris Jones & Genevieve Jolliffe, UK: Cassell, 1996, Paperback, 448 pages, ISBN 0304338540

• *Adventures In The Screen Trade* by William Goldman, UK: Futura, 1990, Paperback, 418 pages, £5.99, ISBN 0708848826

• *Easy Riders, Raging Bulls* by Peter Biskind, UK: Bloomsbury, 1998, Hardback, 506 pages, £20.00, ISBN 0747536309

• *A Pound Of Flesh* by Art Linson, US:Avon, 1995, Paperback, 195 pages, $9.00, ISBN 0380724014

• *Stranger Than Paradise: Maverick Film-Makers In Recent American Cinema* by Geoff Andrew, UK: Prion, 1998, Hardback, 374 pages, £16.99, ISBN 1853752746

• *Filming On A Microbudget* by Paul Hardy, UK: Pocket Essentials, 2001, 96 pages, £3.99, ISBN 190304748X

• *Creative Writing* by Neil Nixon, UK: Pocket Essentials, 2002, 96 pages, £3.99, ISBN 1904048099

Screenwriting Magazines

• *Script*, $6.95 Bimonthly, 5638 Sweet Air Road, Baldwin, MD 21013-0007, USA. www.scriptmag.com

• *Creative Screenwriting*, $6.95 Bimonthly, 6404 Hollywood Blvd, Suite 415, Los Angeles, CA 90028-6261, USA. www.creativescreenwriting.com

• *Scenario*, $20 Quarterly, 104 Fifth Avenue, New York, NY 10011, USA JOHN COSTELLO www.scenariomag.com

• *Scriptwriter* – new UK magazine edited by agent Julian Friedmann. www.scriptwritermagazine.com

◆ ◆ ◆